# *Memoirs of a*
# VAGRANT SOUL
## OR THE PITTED FACE

---

## MIKHAIL NAIMY

## PHILOSOPHICAL LIBRARY
### *New York*

PRINTED IN THE UNITED STATES OF AMERICA
BY HALLMARK - HUBNER PRESS, INC.

# INTRODUCTION

Who is *Pitted Face?*

On a rainy October afternoon, in the year 1916, while passing with a friend through the Syrian quarters in lower Manhattan, a terrific downpour drove us for shelter into a small coffee house inside of which we had never been before.* There wasn't a single customer in the place. We ordered coffee and sat down hoping that the skies would soon shut their sluices, or that the rain would abate to a drizzle.

Presently the proprietor brought us on a tray two cups of Turkish coffee. We were both struck by the way he walked, swaying to the right and to the left as one drunk, or as one walking barefooted on chips of glass. No sooner did he set the cups before us than he dropped to the nearest chair, and letting out a deep sigh, he said,

"Poor Pitted Face! How I miss him . . ."

Seeing two broad question-marks on our faces, he sighed again and continued,

"Ah, this rheumatism. It has well nigh finished me. I didn't mind it so much when Pitted Face was with me. He took care of everything. I would sit all

---

* A coffee house in the East is a place of recreation where people go to while away their leisure hours, to gossip and to air their views over a cup of Turkish coffee, a *narghileh* (water-pipe), a glass of soft or alcoholic drinks, a board of backgammon or checkers, or a deck of cards.

day long, smoke my water-pipe and receive money from my customers. These days I must do the work myself. I must wait on customers and do the chores as well. Don't you know Pitted Face?"

Not waiting to hear our answer, he let out a third sigh and went on mournfully,

"He served here three years,—exactly three full years. He came to me on a day like this, half naked, and with nothing to cover his head. Rain was trickling from his threadbare clothes, a rillet from every thread. I said to him, 'What do you wish, my boy?' And he replied, 'I'm looking for a job.' Said I to myself, 'I'll give him a job as an act of charity, and to please God. Besides, I need a helper. Let me try him out.' Then I put to him the question: 'Would you serve for keep, sonny?' He nodded his consent. Whereupon I took him in, warmed him, fed him and dried his clothes; and he began to work.

"In two or three days he knew about the work as much as I, and more. At the end of the first two months I began to pay him a regular monthly wage of ten dollars plus his room and board. A year later I raised it to fifteen; and a month before he left I gave him another raise of ten dollars. He himself, the poor fellow, never asked for a raise. Never did I hear him complain of anything. He was always contented and worked with his whole heart. Poor Pitted Face. How I miss him!"

The man paused, and it seemed to me that a tear glistened in his eye. I expressed the desire to know his servant's name and his outer descriptions, as perchance I will stumble upon him. But he shook his head dolefully and said,

"If I only knew his name or anything about his family and his circumstances, my heart would not be so sad. He is a short fellow, very thin, and delicate of structure and somewhere between 30 and 35. His hair is black and long. His eyes are large and dark, shaded by heavy eyebrows. His face is pitted with smallpox; therefore we nicknamed him Pitted Face. To anyone who ever asked him about his name, his age, his ancestry, his country, he had but one reply: 'I don't know.' Never did my eye fall on a man so strange, and never shall it fall on one. Is he mad? No. Far from it. He reads and writes Arabic, English, Spanish, French and God knows how many other languages. But you couldn't open his mouth with a crowbar and make him talk. He moved about in utter silence, like a shadow. Yet how quick and precise he was in filling customers' orders and satisfying the slightest of their whims; but always in silence.

"He served in this house three years, and seldom would utter a word above *yes* and *no*. When no customers were about, and no work to be done, he would sit by himself in a corner, take his head between his hands, and stare at the floor before him for an hour, for two, for three at a stretch, barely moving a lash or a muscle, as if nailed to his seat, or as if his eyes were of glass. No, no! A man so strange I have never seen, and shall never see. He would not eat meat or fish. During the first two years of his service here he seldom left the place. Of late only he began to go out."

Our curiosity was aroused to the highest pitch. The desire to know more about that strange servant became uncontrollable, and we asked the man for the address of the house where his servant lived. Straightway he arose and motioned us to follow him. He led us behind a wooden partition in the rear of the shop where he struck a match, and lighting a small gas jet, said,

"Here he lived. Here he passed his nights."

The place was cluttered with wooden and cardboard boxes, and with shelves on which reposed trays, coffee-cups, bottles of all sizes and descriptions. In a corner were three long boards laid across two wooden boxes set about five feet apart. A woolen blanket was spread over the boards with a pillow at one end and a white sheet of muslin showing from under the blanket. This was evidently the cot on which Pitted Face slept. Near the head of the cot were two large wooden cases laid one over the other and covered with Arabic newspapers. An inkwell and a pen testified that the cases so arranged served Pitted Face for a desk. In another corner was a sink and a two-jet gas stove for preparing coffee.

What we saw behind that partition whetted our curiosity more, and we asked the man how long his servant had been gone. For a little over two weeks, he said. As we tried to convince him that there was still hope of his servant's coming back, he shook his head in decided unbelief and said with another deep sigh,

"Pitted Face is dead. Yes, he's dead; so tells me my heart. Were he still living, he would have come back long ago. Poor Pitted Face. How I miss him . . ."

My friend and I stood silent and baffled, not knowing what to do or what to say. Meantime the rain had subsided, and we decided to go. Just as we were leaving, it occurred to me to ask the proprietor if Pitted Face had not left behind him anything in the way of worldly goods outside of his bedding and the inkwell and pen. Whereupon he scratched his head meditatively and quickly disappeared behind the partition, returning a moment later with a small box in his hand.

"This," said he, "is all he left."

Before we said a word he opened the box and took out of it a copy of the New Testament and a writing tablet on whose cover were the following words written in Arabic in a beautiful hand: "From Myself To Myself." There was also a carefully folded foreign newspaper which I recognized as Spanish. Without taking time to look into the book with that strange title, I asked the proprietor if he would sell it, fully prepared to pay him any price he might name. The man fixed me with two bewildered eyes and said,

"Sell it? Is it a jewel that I would ask a price for it? It is but a tablet for writing. Take it with my compliments. Its owner,—peace be to his soul,—is

ix

gone never to return. So tells me my heart. As to me, I neither read nor write. Take it, Mister; take it. But do drop in now and then. The place is yours. Come again."

We wished the man well, and departed. I could hardly wait to get home and read the book in my hand.

Now that I have read these memoirs time and again, and that years have rolled by since their author's mysterious disappearance, I feel no scruples about letting others share with me the rare pleasure I gleaned from their pages. As to the author's peculiar way of recording the days of the week without any reference to the date, the month, and the year,—on that I have no comments to offer.

That is all I know of Pitted Face and his memoirs. Ask me for no more.                                   **M. N.**

# MEMOIRS OF A VAGRANT SOUL

# THE MEMOIRS

*Monday*

Broadly speaking, all men may be divided into two categories: Those who talk, and those who keep their peace.

I am the silent part of humanity. The rest are all talkers. As for the sucklings and the dumb, their lips have been sealed for a reason by Eternal Wisdom. Whereas I have set a seal on my own lips with my own hand; for I have tasted the passing sweetness of Silence, while those who talk are too drunk with the gall of talking to be sobered up with the kiss of Silence.

Therefore do I keep my peace while others talk.

3

*Wednesday*

I am a recluse among men.

To be a recluse among men is much more trying than to be a recluse among beasts. For with little love and kindliness you may win a beast's confidence and affection. And even if you fail in that you risk nothing but your skin. Whereas with men love is often seen as a bait, and kindliness as a sign of weakness. They would avoid causing a scratch to your perishable skin because of laws they have enacted for the purpose; while they would smear with slime and tear to shreds your imperishable soul, and no laws or courts can prevent them from doing it. Therefore have I left my body as a target for their tongues, and fenced my soul with silence.

They saw the traces of smallpox upon my face, and nicknamed me Pitted Face. But for my soul which is wrapped in silence and far beyond the reach of their blind eyes they found no name. Hence I appear to them as an idiot. Yet from behind my veil of silence I can look into their hearts and minds and read them like a book. For I judge them not by what they say, but by that which they leave unsaid.

Therefore do I keep my peace while others talk.

4

*Thursday*

"That's not what I mean."

How it pains me to hear people sometimes speak with vehemence and sincerity and then turn to their auditor, or auditors, and say, "That's not what I mean."

Were I given the power I would put these words, —"That's not what I mean,"—at the end of every book ever written by a writer; of every poem ever composed by a poet; of every speech ever delivered by an orator; I would engrave them on every statue ever chiselled by a sculptor, and every picture ever painted by an artist. And why? Because all human modes of expression, no matter how fine and how sincere, are too narrow to contain men's thoughts and emotions. Though they know it not, all men are yet but lisping babes.

As to these memoirs, though not written for men, I shall put at their end, "That's not what I mean."

Intention is the only index to veracity. Yet to express an intention is to put on it a mask. Therefore are men in constant pain endeavoring to sift the true in their speech from the untrue. As to me,—the silent part of humanity,—how can I lie? Expression

5

only can deceive. Intentions, whether good or bad, are never lies so long as left unmasked.

Speech is a mixture of truth and untruth. While Silence is truth unadulterated.

Therefore do I keep my peace while others talk.

### Friday

The severest punishment for a liar is to believe his lies.

### Saturday

I am an obscure, insignificant, uncomely man, with a smallpox-pitted face. So I appear to men; and that is all they know about me. Why does not that suffice them? When they call to me, "Pitted Face, give us 5 coffees, or 3 whiskies, or a poker deck and chips," is not that all they need of me? Why, then, do they importune me with questions about my name, my father's and mother's names, my country, my ancestry, etc., etc.? Would I cease to be obscure, insignificant and uncomely if I were to tell them that I was the son of some lord or millionaire?

I have no name, and refuse to be known by a single name. For I am a new man each time a new thought is born in me; and my thoughts are born much faster than I can glimpse them. If I be David now, I am Solomon, or Samson, or Abraham in another instant. It is what I think, rather than what I appear, that determines who I am. And my mind is never still. Like wind it dashes here and there; and as the wind that passes over green meadows brings me the fragrance of meadows; or the stench of dungheaps when passing over dungheaps, so does my mind bring me constantly new odors, images and shadows from its bewildering excursions into new worlds and realms.

So long as I am a mind endowed with a body, rather than a body endowed with a mind; and so long as my mind bubbles with images and thoughts as bubbles effervescent water in a glass, just so long will I be a new man each twinkling of an eye. Whereas my body, so slow to change, continues to appear to men as if it were one and the same. Therefore am I Pitted Face, and shall so remain until I cast off this garment and put on another, or—as men say —until I die.

People are in need of names to keep their silly records, to run their puny courts and governments, to set rules for their conduct towards each other so that I—Pitted Face—would know that yonder garden

was the property of John Doe, and I had no right to
touch an onion therein even if I were famished; and
that the house across belonged to Richard Roe, and
I would not be permitted to seek shelter within it
even if I were to perish from cold outside.

I wonder what would happen to people if they
were to wake up some morning and find their memories entirely vacant of names,—their own and those
of others. Would not their lives be paralyzed because
their records became paralyzed? What confusion!
What Chaos! And why? Because people live by names
and for names, rather than live for Life and by Life.
To strike a man's name off their records is tantamount
with them to striking him off the records of Life.

Shall people ever come to know that all their
records are but so much scribbling on the sand of
the seashore? What they record of themselves is of
no moment; it is what Life records of them that
counts, for that is preserved unto the end of Time.
And Life records their every wish and thought; their
every sound and sigh; their every tear and smile; their
every word and deed. Nothing is lost; nothing is
overlooked in Life's archives. There are neither names,
nor passports in Life's fearfully accurate, meticulous
and painstaking records. There are but sharp and
deep imprints of deeds, thoughts, sentiments and purposes, hidden or manifest; all similar to the eyes of
men, yet quite dissimilar to the eyes of the great

keepers of Life's book of records who readily distinguish between them as does a veteran criminologist distinguish between one man's fingerprints and another's.

I am to-day in K.P.'s* and his customers' eyes just Pitted Face,—a nameless, obscure, insignificant and uncomely man whose only use in this world is to serve others with coffee, whisky, poker paraphernalia, to wash cups and saucers, to sweep and to dust this place. Were I to tell them to-morrow that my name was lord, or prince So-and-So, the scales would instantly be turned. They would become the servants and I, the master.

Let men record the names and deeds of men. But I,—the silent part of humanity,—am quite content with what the Fates record of me in the great Book of Life.

Therefore do I keep my peace while others talk.


### Saturday


When will this trembling leave me?
My whole body is like a machine whose screws

---

* It is clear from the text that the initials K. P. refer to the proprietor.

and springs have been set loose. I have lost control
of all my muscles. The hands shake; the teeth click;
the heart bounces and flutters like a bird in a cage;
the lungs are about to blow up. In vain, in vain I try
to write.

Who is she? And why? Better to . . .

No, no! This is more than I can bear. What does
this young woman seek of me? And who is she? I fled
the Argentine to be rid of her. Who told her that I
was in New York, and who led her to my hermitage?

I sat me down to write after all the customers had
gone; and they did not leave till 2 o'clock past midnight. I lit the gas and took up the pen; but my hand
became of a sudden stiff and lifeless. I felt I was not
alone. A shiver went up and down my spine, and
the hair bristled on my head. I tried to look back,
but could not; to the right or left, and again could
not. The blood almost froze in my veins. I made an
effort to rise, but in vain; to open my mouth, but also
in vain. Then I became as cold and stiff as a stone.
Finally I managed to turn to the right, and I saw
her . . .

Again the shiver seizes me. My fingers would not
obey me. I must rest.

She is still the same. Nothing has changed in her
since she appeared to me the first time. That gaping
wound in her throat is still unhealed. Blood flows
from it as before. That deep, immobile, fearful sad-

ness in her large eyes is still as deep, as immobile and as fearful as before. Her long black tresses still cascade over her shoulders. Her breasts protrude as before from under her white, transparent silk gown. Her delicate left hand grasps the wound in her throat as if trying to stay the flow of blood. Her face is like ivory,—pale and bloodless. But her eyes . . . Oh! Her eyes! I looked at them, and it appeared to me as if all the pains and the sorrows of humanity were staring at me from behind their lashes. They do not move; but they are deeper than the deepest deeps. Nor revenge, nor bitterness can be seen in them; but sorrow without end, and a question, or rather a supplication . . . What does she pray of me? What can I do for her?

How awesome is deep, silent sorrow! And this woman appears to me as the very personification of deep, silent sorrow. So much so that if she were to open her mouth, a flood of sorrow would gush out of her eyes. Perhaps, her sight then would not make me tremble. But she is silent; and her silence overawes me. I am silent; but my silence awes no one. Hers is an awesome, mystifying silence.

How long she stood by my side,—a moment, an hour, an eternity,—I could not tell. As she appeared suddenly, so she disappeared, leaving me limp and broken up as one fallen from the talons of an eagle high in the sky.

How strange! Each time this woman visits me a thick fog envelops my mind. Stranger still is that the longer she stays, the finer and the more transparent the fog becomes. And the feeling grips me strongly of some kinship between her and me,—as if I had seen her before; as if I knew her; as if there was some tie that bound me to her. At times I almost remember where I saw her, how I came to know her, and the tie that binds me to her. Just as the veil appears to be lifting, I look for her and find her not.

Be patient, Pitted Face. Patience and Silence will in the end unlock all doors before you.


*Sunday*

Silence.


*Monday*

Silence.


*Tuesday*

Silence.

12

*Wednesday*

My soul has been longing of late for the Brides of Night; and no aperture in this hermitage to serve me for a peep-hole into the world outside. Even if there was one, I could not see through it a single star. For the hand of man has done its utmost in this city to shut the firmament away from his eyes.

The longing was so strong and overpowering that I walked out of the place to-night without saying a word to K. P. I wanted the company of the sea and the stars. Forgetting that I was a servant in a coffee house, I made straight for the shore, and there sent my eyes seaward and skyward.

"Having eyes, they see not; and having ears, they hear not." How little, in fact, do men see and hear! They passed by me by the hundreds; their eyes on the tips of their shoes; their ears dinning with the prattle of their tongues that never tire of hashing and re-hashing their childish hopes and wants, their petty pains and pleasures.

I heard one say, "What a beautiful night!" meaning that it was neither hot nor cold, for most men measure nature by the thermometer. Another said,

13

"How glorious the stars!" yet were his eyes upon the ground between his feet.

The stars and I are a teacher and a pupil. In them I see the glory of God, and from them I learn my insignificance as a mold of clay, and my majesty as God's living likeness and image.

The stars and I are two infinite worlds that merge in one vast, boundless world called Pitted Face,— this very obscure, insignificant, and uncomely man.

Men look at stars with their eyes, and therefore see them not. Stars must be looked at with pious hearts, and in reverential silence.

Therefore do I keep my peace while others talk.

### Saturday

Barely had K.P. opened the door and seen me in the morning when he began to shower me with the vilest curses:

"Where in hell were you last night, you damnable Pitted Face? Why did you go and leave me, you fatherless and motherless rat? You shall be my undoing. You shall ruin my house. Cursed be that hour in which I first laid eyes on your owlish face. It serves me right. That is what I get for taking pity

14

on you; for warming you, feeding you, giving you work and lodging, and wages to boot. How did you leave me alone seeing how stiff with rheumatism I am? Where did you stray? Where did you bury yourself last night?" etc., etc.

What could I tell him in return? Could I say to one whose main preoccupation in life is to draw money from the pockets of others into his that I was seized with an uncontrollable longing to see the stars and the sea? How could I make him understand that to commune with the sea and the stars was an occupation incomparably more profitable than serving coffee and drinks to customers in return for so much of their money?

To limit the needs of the body is a virtue. To limit the needs of the soul is a sin.

The case with K.P. is reversed. The night he has no gamblers in his place he becomes fidgety and irritable. His moustaches droop, his face becomes sallow, his cheeks fallen, his eyes cloudy, and his rheumatic pains quite unendurable. He sits to one side grim and forlorn, the very embodiment of ill luck and desolation. His family budget suddenly swells up, his overhead expenses almost double, and all his world cares in general become unsupportable. The night, however, he sees in his place a goodly company of men engaged in gambling away their monies and their lives and in burying deep the talents

15

given them by God, his face lights up with a broad smile, the corners of his moustaches get twisted upward, his eyes press forward out of their sockets, his rheumatic pains disappear, and his family budget and other world worries dwindle to naught. Then he takes his water-pipe, and crossing his legs on a chair in the corner, begins giving orders: "Take this, Pitted Face. Bring that, Pitted Face."

As to K. P.'s customers, it seems that the Almighty has made them of clay and forgot to blow of his spirit into them; with the exception of Sennacherib. That is the name by which he is known in this house; whether it is a nickname or a real one,—I don't know. I found some affinity between that man and myself. More than once I felt inclined to speak to him, but restrained myself.

The man walks and behaves like an enigma. Every time I look at him I feel as if I am looking at a great question mark. He is a constant customer of this house. Since I came to this place he has not missed a single night. Neither heat, nor hail, nor sleet would deter him from coming. He walks in every evening about eight o'clock, greets K. P., takes a chair and sits by the window, orders coffee, lights a cigarette, then opens the newspaper he invariably brings with him and digs his long, aquiline nose into its pages, to lift it only when called by some customer, "What about a game of poker, Sennacherib?" Then he rises languidly, takes a chair by the poker table, and there sits for hours deeply absorbed in the game and rarely opening his mouth. Only when his companions decide to quit playing will he leave the table and walk out apparently unmindful of any gain or loss.

He is sparing of words. His voice is low and barely audible; his movements are slow, deliberate and sluggish; his complexion is waxen, his face is so thin one would think his cheeks were drawn together by a thread inside the mouth; his fingers are long, lean and bony; his clothes are old and with more than one button missing. As to his eyes, they are lit with a light like that of the moon,—pale, calm, cold, deep and sad. I carefully observe his every move and endeavor to engage his attention. But he comes and goes and pays no heed to me, as if I did not exist for him. Customers like to poke fun at him, but he meets their shafts with extreme unconcern and even shares sometimes in their fun.

For some reason I find solace in Sennacherib's presence, even if I be in no need of any solace from men.

### Friday

Said the fool in his heart, "There is no God."
Verily, a fool's god is his foolishness.

17

I wonder what Sennacherib says. I felt like asking him the question to-day, but refrained.

Since it is in man's nature to deny what he does not know, why does he not deny himself? It is the height of folly for men to seek knowledge through the outer senses alone which can never penetrate beyond the outer shell of things. Being limited and bounded, they set to all things boundaries and limits; whereas the slightest thing is limitless and boundless. So easily deceived, their verdicts can be but deceptions.

The senses that rely neither on eye nor ear; neither on nose, nor tongue, nor hand,—such senses are nonsense in the code of men. Should you say to them that they had eyes invisible to their eyes, and ears of finer substance than flesh and blood, and that in silent contemplation they could see what the outer eye is incapable of seeing, and hear what the outer ear is powerless to hear,—should you say that to them, they would dub you on the instant a fool, or a lunatic. How shall one who hears what men cannot hear, and sees what men cannot see, be aught but a fool or a lunatic in the eyes of men?

Much speaking is a distraction to the mind. Yet men are garrulous beyond all bounds. Nothing oppresses them so much as to be silent and to meditate. How, then, do they hope to find God in themselves? How do they speak the name of God not having found Him themselves? Verily, they speak only a hollow word,—a name that designates no one. Did they but know God indeed, they should not have made of Him so many gods: a Hebrew god; a Christian god; a Mohammedan god; a Buddhist god; a heathen god. They should not have shed each other's blood, nor hated one another in the name of God and for the sake of God. Nor should they have been divided and subdivided into so many creeds and sects. But they are so divided and subdivided, and hate and fight one another, because they have attempted the impossible in attempting to define the undefinable, and to limit the illimitable in their various tongues, so limited and so confined.

Men shall continue to hate in the name of God, and to spill blood for the sake of God until they come to know Him in reverential silence and humble meditation. Then shall they be able to commune without words, to have their minds under perfect control, and with well-controlled minds to move mountains and to lift the seas upon the wings of air.

Does Sennacherib meditate on God in his silence? Or is he silent for reasons that have nothing to do with God?

### Thursday

Day of silence.

Had I the power over men, I would decree that all the peoples of the earth observe one day at least of every year as a Day of Silence. On that day they shall be made to muzzle their tongues, and to devote their hearts and minds to meditation. But there be nations so given to gossip, and with tongues so loose; for them I would decree a whole month of silence.

### Sunday

To-day I put to myself the question: "Who are you, Pitted Face?"

The answer was a long, deep silence.

I am a man; and as such I must have been born of a father and a mother. Who is my father? Who is my mother?

Did a woman bear me for nine months, then feed me with her breasts? Did she wake nights over my cradle, singing me lullabies and warming me with the affections of her heart? Did she call me by a certain name, and what was that name? Did her eyes moisten with tears when she lost me? Is she thinking of me this very minute, and praying that I may return to her? Does she know, or does she wish to know, where I am? Where is she,—in this world or beyond it? Who is the woman I may call my mother?

People glorify the mother to the point of deifying her. They are unhappy when away from her, and shed bitter tears when death carries her away from them. But here is a man who has no mother, and whose heart does not contract in pain because he finds himself without a mother. I am I,—with or without a mother. And I am I,—with or without a father.

Behold a strange phenomenon: I call aloud, Mother, Mother, Mother! and Father, Father, Father!, yet my heart remains calm and unmoved. Not a string of joy or sorrow vibrates therein. Was I, perchance, not born of a father and a mother?

And where was I born?

People call their place of birth their Country, or their Native Land, and surround it with a halo of sanctity. They languish with nostalgia when away from it, and shed their blood to defend its soil against invaders. And why? Only because they have grown accustomed to it. A Country, then, is but a habit with those who inhabit it. And men have ever been the slaves of their habits. Therefore have they divided the Earth into small corrals which they call their Countries or Native Lands. "This is *my* country, and that is *yours*. Keep within the boundaries of your country, and dare not transgress the boundaries of mine. For if you do, I will make the sword the arbiter between us." So speak men of one corral to men of another corral. And the sword has been mowing their heads ever since they became enslaved to the habit of clinging to one Country, and to a fetish called Patriotism.

Tahasaki was born in the Islands of the Rising Sun, of a Japanese father and a Japanese mother. Therefore is he Japanese, and Japan his native land. Therefore, also, is his world divided in two parts: Japan and not-Japan; and Japan is by far the better and the more important part.

But Hung Li Kai was born in China of a Chinese father and a Chinese mother. Therefore is China his native land, and his world divided in two parts: China, and not-China; and China is by far the better and the more important part.

Ivan Bourjinsky, on the other hand, was born in Russia of Russian parents. Therefore is Russia his native land, and his world is divided in two parts: Russia and not-Russia; and Russia is by far the better and the more important part.

Likewise one may speak of all the other peoples of the earth.

But I,—the silent part of humanity,—I do not know, and little care to know, where I was born and of whom. Therefore am I a man without a country. Even if I had one, I would renounce it. With the Universe for my home I would not be confined to the earth; much less to a fraction thereof. Were the whole earth mine, and were some pigmy from the Black Continent to claim a foot thereof, I would gladly surrender to him the rest.

Not so Tahasaki. For if he owned the whole earth except a foot owned by Hung Li Kai, he would fight Hung Li Kai for that foot and justify himself on "patriotic" grounds.

### Monday

Behold! The peoples of the earth are engaged in a war the like of which, they say, the earth has never witnessed before. They die by the millions the most horrible of deaths. And why? Has the earth suddenly contracted that there is no longer room for all of them? God forbid. Their hearts, their minds, their imaginations have contracted to the point of believing that by expanding the boundaries of their countries they would expand as well the boundaries of their crammed and stuffy souls.

The earth is still the earth. Men can neither add to it, nor subtract from it so much as a grain of sand. And never has the earth been such a foolish mother as to give birth to more than she could feed. Rather are men the fools who, having a common heritage in the earth, insist on partitioning their heritage, and till this day are wrangling over the shares. Not to appear as dogs ferociously tearing each other's hides over a bone, they have invented such screens for their ferocity as "Native Country," "National Pride," "Patriotism," "Freedom" and the like.

It has always been so with men. They would spill each other's blood in the name of a flatulent abstraction such as national honor and national pride.

Men go to war, yet hate it with all their hearts and souls. And therein is a riddle. War to them is a great evil, but an unavoidable one. And war is evil in their eyes because of the blood it sheds, and the buildings it demolishes, and the wealth it dissipates, and the pain and sorrow it causes to the combatants, as well as to the noncombatants. Would those were the only sins of war! For nature has a way of always replenishing her depleted stores, whether of flesh and blood; whether of health and wealth; as she has

24

a way of embalming sorrow with the balm of forget-
fulness.

Evil, indeed, it is,—and a great one,—to shatter
a living body. But the greater evil by far is to shatter
a living soul. And that is the crying evil and the
hideous crime War perpetrates alike on those who go
to war and those who stay behind.

Thus War says to Von Schuster:

"Listen, my dear Von Schuster. You know nothing
about yourself, about your God, or about the reason
for which you were born. You lie, Von Schuster, and
gossip, and deceive. You covet your neighbor's wife
and possessions, and kill, and steal, and commit adultery in thought and in deed. You also gamble, and
drink, and beat your wife. You have a large family
and no means to support them; and you are tortured
in mind and body because of that; so much so that I
often heard you curse the hour of your birth and
wish you were not born. Never mind, Von Schuster;
these are all trifles. What imports is the fact that you
were born in Munich. Therefore you are German
before all else, and Germany is your country. As a
good German you, no doubt, love your country with
the flaming love of a patriot.

"Do you know who your enemy is, Von Schuster?
It is not ignorance, nor drunkenness, nor gossip, nor
deceit, nor adultery, nor weak will; nor is it poverty
that causes you so much pain and melancholy. No, it is

none of these. Your *real* enemy is Jean Jardinier, who was not born in Munich, nor in Leipzig, nor in Baden-Baden, but beyond your country's western boundary. And what is more, he neither speaks your tongue, nor eats what you eat, nor dresses as you dress. And furthermore, his face is not as blond as your face. That, my dear Von Schuster, is your enemy. So draw your sword and chop his head off his shoulders. Then shall happiness descend on you in a basket from the sky."

So speaks War to Jean Jardinier of Von Schuster, and to Bourjinsky of Tahasaki, and to Tahasaki of Hung Li Kai. And so the dupes spring on each other's throats. Their blood flows in streams; their dwellings tumble on their heads; their hearts and skulls are cracked; their wives are widowed, and their children orphaned. And he who butchers more men, demolishes more homes, and renders more wives widows, and more children orphans, War proclaims him a hero, sets him on a pedestal, covers his chest with ornaments of honor, fills his coffers with lucre, and his ears with handclapping and vociferous acclaim, while manliness, veracity, integrity, charity, and love of peace and life, all too noble to afflict a living man with pain, are left to wander in the earth unseen, unheard, unheralded and despised.

War's most hideous crime is the distortion of truth and the reversal of values. It enthrones savagery as

26

heroism. The man who can conquer and subdue a brother-man it honors and exalts. The man too busy conquering and subduing the savage and the beast in himself, that he may love and help his fellow-men, it brands as a coward and a "slacker."

In K. P.'s and in his customers' eyes I am a coward. For every day I suffer at their hands so many insults which, if addressed to another, would infuriate him and cause him to draw a dagger, or to use his fists right and left in defense of his "honor". But I would not be tricked away from my fight with a stubborn enemy within by enemies without, too weak to deserve a blow, or even a word. As to my *honor*, it is beyond the reach of men's hands and tongues. No matter how they vilify me, I remain as distant from their abuse as is my mind from their minds.

Therefore do I keep my peace while others talk.

### Tuesday

I saw to-day on the seashore a young maiden sitting on a rock. I sat on a rock opposite, and we began to converse.

I asked the maiden, but in silence: "What do you do here, my maiden?"

She answered me, also in silence: "People are bathing in the sea, but I am bathing in my sorrows."

Said I, again in silence: "What makes you so sorrowful, my maiden?"

And she replied in silence: "Long have I sought a youth on whom to bestow my love; but I found none. And now my love is withered and is turned into gall. The heart that once so overflowed with love is now a sea whose shores are of salt, and whose waters are of gall."

Whereupon I terminated the colloquy and bowed my head very low before that bitter sea.

Then I turned to my heart and said: "What is love, my heart?" But there came no answer. Yet my heart is not a sea whose shores are of salt, and whose waters are of gall.

*Wednesday*

I have a companion who shares with me my lodging and my board. Like myself he is a silent hermit, detached from the members of his own clan. We have grown accustomed and attached to each other. He accepts neither caress nor food from any

28

other hand but mine. When he sees me busy, he sits to one side and follows with his eyes every move I make. When he sees me sitting and meditating, he approaches softly and slowly, and begins making circles around me, trying all the while to catch my eye with his eye. If he detects the slightest sign of welcome in my eye, he jumps to my lap, curls up in the shape of a cruller, covers his face with his hands, and begins to purr contentedly. That is his way of reminding me of himself and of entreating me not to cast him out of my mind.

If I happen to leave the place, I invariably find him on coming back awaiting me behind the door. No sooner do I step inside than he runs towards me and blocks the way rubbing himself against my leg as if to say, "I'm here, and glad that you are back." I take him up and hug him. Then he shuts his eyes coquettishly and surrenders completely to his cattish bliss.

I surprised him to-day and found him standing in the middle of the room with a giant rat dangling from his mouth, his teeth sunk into the poor rat's neck. Contrary to his habit, he did not move an inch to meet me, but remained fixed in his pose, his legs far apart, his eyes glassy and wide-open, and the rat squirming, and twisting, and vainly grasping the air for something to take a hold of. When exhausted by useless kicking and writhing, the rat would give up

all effort, resignedly shut its eyes, and let its body
fall limp and straight with a good part of the long
tail resting on the ground. Having rested a brief
moment, it would once more go the round of the
same pathetic, useless motions.

I stood and watched the rat's unequal battle with
my companion and felt as if watching the first murder
ever committed on earth. I felt the very veins of my
heart attached to the rat's feet and hands. My heartbeats quickened or slackened as the movements of
the rat's feet and hands quickened or slackened. When
the rat breathed its last, and my companion walked
away to consummate his crime behind the wooden
boxes in the corner, the breath almost stopped in my
nostrils, and the air became oppressively heavy.

When I gained control of myself I looked towards
the corner and saw my erstwhile companion emerge
from behind the wooden cases licking his chops and
walking deliberately in my direction as if hesitating
to approach me, not knowing whether I would receive
him like a hero, or like a criminal. Finally he decided
to probe my feelings in the matter, and approaching
shyly, began, as was his wont, to walk in circles about
me, but without daring to look me in the eye.
Having circled for a while without winning so much
as a sympathetic glance from me, he slunk away,
puzzled and heavy-hearted, to ponder in his solitude
the mystery of my cold behavior towards him.

My companion is not the first cat to devour a rat. Nor is that rat the first of its tribe to be torn with the teeth of a cat. Why, then, did that rat's death shake me so profoundly and turn my heart away from my companion? Was not what my companion did in keeping with "God's will and the laws of nature"?

Yea, it is the will of God; but only in things and creatures below the state of man. It is God's will for cats and rats, but not for man. Otherwise, why my disgust and my nausea at my companion's deed? Why do men and women shudder, and sometimes faint, at the sight of bloodshed? Why do their laws condemn murder as a crime?

A wealthy business man strangles a poor competitor by all the ruses known to business and to wealth. And men declare, "It is the will of God and a law of Nature. Does not the cat strangle the mouse?"

A man deprives another man of the breath and beauty of life. And people shake their heads wisely and say, "It is the will of God and a law of Nature. Does not the wolf deprive the lamb of the breath and beauty of life?"

A powerful nation swallows up a weak one. And people wash their hands of the crime and say, "That is the will of God and a law of Nature. Does not the snake swallow the toad?"

Is there no difference between God's image and a cat? Between God's likeness and a wolf, or a snake?

31

In vain men hide their shame behind the example of the cat and rat. Have they not found out yet that death is the wages of hiding from the face of Life?

Death is death to the creator of death, who is man. But God, who is Life,—how can He be the author and the source of death?

### Thursday

Never since I came to live and to move among people did I see the face of a man so crushed and so despondent as K. P.'s face this morning.

He walked into the place as one who had just witnessed the greatest catastrophe that ever struck the world since the Deluge. One looking at him would have thought that the sun had suddenly blown up; that the moon and stars had vanished from the skies; that the sea had overrun the land, and left not a breath of air anywhere; that waters everywhere had been turned to blood, and all living beings, excepting him and me, had been swallowed up by Chaos. All because the bank where he kept his savings of $3,000 has failed! . . .

32

"Three thousand dollars, Pitted Face. Three thousand dollars! Fifteen years of my life squandered in scraping them together,—the labor of countless wakeful nights and feverish days,—all gone in a jiffy,— gone, gone, gone. Lost is my home. Lost is my life. Lost are my children. All, all is lost. A large family is tied to my neck. Wherewith shall I feed and clothe them? God, O my God! Destroy the homes of those who destroyed my home. Let gold in their hands turn into dust, and the bread in their mouths into stones, and the clothes on their backs into scorpions and vipers. Three thousand dollars, Pitted Face, three thousand—gone like a puff of wind, never to return. May the scoundrels themselves go like a puff of wind."

As he bemoaned his lot, he would rub his hands, slap his face, gnash his teeth, pull his hair, strike the floor with a chair, fall into convulsions and sob like a babe. I began to suspect that the man had lost his wits. The suspicion became almost a conviction when he rushed towards me, and grabbing me violently by the shoulders, began to shake me and to roar:

"Say something. Don't stand around like a dumb-bell. Curse with me the villains who were the cause of my ruin; may you, too, be ruined. Speak. Waggle your lazy tongue with at least one curse. Gone is the coffee house. Gone is the money. Gone are we all and trampled under hoofs. Three thousand; three thousand dollars, Pitted Face. The bloody sweat of fifteen years,—a lifetime; all gone, gone, gone. Gone also are your wages of ten dollars a month. Would you work from now on for keep and no more? If so, stay. Otherwise look for a job elsewhere."

When I learned the cause of his distress and was assured that the world was still intact and doing its usual rounds, I smiled in my heart at the fact that his first impulse was to cut off my monthly allowance. Let him keep it with my compliments.

How pitiful and painful at once that a family of seven souls should not be worth in the scales of human values any more than three thousand dollars in the bank! If the bank fails, that family also fails. Seven gods for $3,000! How very cheap! And there be images of God on the earth who are worth nothing at all because they are penniless and do not own an inch of land, or a peg in a wall. Yet people wonder why their life, founded on such delusive, ephemeral values, is so delusive and ephemeral. To build life on money, on possessions, on buying and selling, on profit and loss, is to build it on shifting sands. Life is not a trade. It is a giving and a taking; and the foundation of it is God.

As I work for keep, so must all people work. The strong should be made to provide for the young, the old, the infirm, and the disabled. Then is mankind a single family, and the earth the family-store and

34

larder. Then shall men spend but a fraction of their time on the body and the needs thereof; the rest they shall devote to their souls.

To buy and sell is to trade life away for a pittance,—a diamond for a piece of glass.

To give and take with a large heart is to enter the portals of Love, Peace and Immortality.

*Friday*

Rare is the man who, having suffered some misfortune, would blame it on himself instead of blaming it on fate, on time or on other men.

All happenings in the world are timed with infinite precision as are the movements of the earth and stars, the steady march of seasons, and the succession of nights and days. As fruits and seeds have their time for ripening; and animals and human beings their periods of gestation, so do thoughts, deeds, hopes, feelings, words, intentions have their seasons for ripening and their periods of gestation. When the time is at hand they are delivered of their burden which may be a tear or a smile; a blessing or a curse; a kiss or a bite; a fortune or a calamity. But people are blissfully unconscious of most of their thoughts, emotions and deeds. Therefore do they stand aghast at what those thoughts, emotions, and deeds so often beget them.

There is K.P.,—and all men are K.P.'s; he blames heaven and earth for the loss of his savings, but blames not himself. Yet he alone is to blame.

And there be men with pretentions to piety who, when in trouble, would console themselves with the thought that God in His lovingkindness had "visited" them "to try" their faith. The dupes! God never *tries* anyone. God teaches and instructs. They only try and test who cannot tell in advance the result of the trial and the test.

Yea, God instructs those who believe and those who believe not. With Him the noble and the ignoble, the faithful and the faithless, the clean and the unclean are equally worthy of attention. And He instructs them all, now by pleasure, now by pain; now by giving, now by withholding. There is no end to His patience and the variety of His lessons. Slowly, but readily, He helps men up the ladder of knowledge that they may finally come to know His will in them and their destiny in Him.

To absorb one lesson well is worth a whole lifetime. To learn, say, that money is worthless as a foundation on which to build a life; that the deed ever rebounds on the doer, is to reap a good harvest, and to pave the way for learning other lessons. A lesson well understood is never repeated; while one misunderstood is repeated again and again in diverse forms and manners until its meaning sinks in the mind and the heart. And because men are slow to learn, their life is so unbalanced and so full of trouble. Until to-day they have not learned that to seek refuge from pain in pleasure is to reap more pain; and to skip a hard lesson is only to come to a harder one. They have not yet found out that the only way to escape pain is to know what the Great Teacher requires of them, and to do it well.

*Saturday*

Why has it been decreed for you, Pitted Face, at this juncture of your life, to be a servant in a coffee house? And where? In New York! Why has it fallen to your lot to mix with coffee house devotees; to hear their filthy jabbering; to witness their frequent squabbles, and to cater to their whims?

Therein is more than one lesson for you to learn, Pitted Face. Be awake, and learn well.

37

*Wednesday*

The light of a match,—the light of a candle,—the light of an electric projector,—the light of the sun. One light; one source.

Blessed be that Light whence issues every light, and which no darkness can overcome. Within me, O Light inextinguishable, is a spark from your holy forge. How it longs to be united with you and to be lost in you!

*Thursday*

Noah!

Did it ever occur to the conqueror of the Flood that, thousands of years after his death, his name would be the cause of a hot scuffle in a Syrian coffee-house in New York?

Two customers with some pretentions to learning had an argument to-day as to whether *Noah* in a certain Arabic sentence was a subject or a predicate.

The argument became so heated that saucers, cups and even chairs began to fly about. The result was that Sennacherib who ventured to play the role of the peacemaker was hit with a chair and, swaying like one drunk, fell to the ground, blood gushing from a wound in his head.

I do not recall what happened after; for the sight of flowing blood made me faint. When I came to, I found myself in bed with darkness thick and ominous all about. Until to-night I have not felt the need of a companion. But now the stillness about me seems to lie heavy on my chest. The only companion of my solitude has disappeared since he killed the rat. How I wish he would come back to-night. I am ready to forgive him all his sins.

### Friday

Sennacherib is in the hospital; while he who would make *Noah* a predicate, and he who would make him a subject are both in prison. And Noah is still Noah.

How quick are men to disagree; how very slow to agree. One can hardly think of anything which was not, at some time, the cause of quarreling between one or more human beings. The saddest part in any quarrel or dispute is that both parties claim to be defending the "right" or the "truth."

When shall men realize that Right and Truth have never been in need of defenders, nor have they ever been the cause of splitting men apart! It is Falsehood only, whose feet are of clay, that needs to be propped and defended and is always the cause of quarrelling among its own defenders.

To quarrel over a rule of grammar or syntax,— how ridiculous! Did the language make the man, or the man the language? Is not the language a tool created by man for his own convenience and comfort? When the tool becomes the master of its maker, pity the maker and the tool.

The perfect language has not yet been found, nor shall it ever be found so long as men depend on words and rules for self-expression. A rule is a welcome necessity when used to clarify the meaning and to render the art of communicating emotions and ideas quick, simple, and effective. When it becomes a cumbrance to the memory, a hindrance to the hand, and a nettle to the tongue, then it is high time to consign it to an ignominious end with all the litter and trash of history. Such rules are still abundant in every human tongue, and are the bane of school boys and girls, of writers and poets, of orators and men of affairs all over the world. Yet do the nations of the world cling tenaciously to those ugly warts and pernicious cancers in their various tongues.

The richest and the most decorous of languages is the poorest in rules and the simplest in structure. Such is the language of telepathy, to which all the other languages are but stepping-stones and ladders. The more complex and intricate its rules, the farther is the language from the top of the ladder. The fewer the rules and the less involved, the nearer the language to the top.

Woe to the people who never change, nor allow their language to change in a constantly changing world. Such people are like a stagnant pool to which the floods and winds carry all manners of filth and disintegration.

### Sunday

Time and I are a steed and a rider. It cannot outstrip me, nor can I outstrip it. When we reach the goal, we shall be neither a steed, nor a rider.

I pity those who are always rushing headlong as if in a race with Time and seriously intent on leaving it leagues and leagues behind. Such racers invariably end where they start. Breathless, exhausted and broken up, they drop in their tracks, while Time marches on. More deserving of pity are those who insist on carrying Time on their backs, proclaiming all the while that "Time is money." How crushing is their burden!

### Monday

To hesitate in any action is to be uncertain and afraid of the results of that action. And that is a decided weakness. What matters the result when the purpose is honest and clean? What man is so clear of sight as to follow the devious course of any act unto the end of Time?

I was undecided yesterday about whether or not to visit Sennacherib in the hospital. Finally I decided to make the visit.

As I opened the door of his ward, I found him reclining in bed and reading a newspaper; his head heavily bandaged, and by his side a small table with various bottles. I stood for a while in the doorway not knowing what to do and quite unable to force my tongue to speak, even to the extent of mumbling a simple greeting. Finally I took a few steps forward

42

hoping that he would read in my eyes the unspoken greeting and compassion I held for him in my heart. Quite independently from my will and from the rest of my body, my hand stretched forward to grasp his hand. But he made me withdraw it quickly when he fixed me with an icy look, and turning his head away from me in great disgust, pressed an electric button. To the nurse who responded to his call he said gruffly and without looking at me, "Put this man out at once."

Very much puzzled I retraced my steps. Was Sennacherib ashamed of my face and my shabby clothes? Or did a sudden attack of pain make it impossible for him to talk to any one? Let him think of me and do to me whatever he may please. I shall continue to think well of him and give him room in my heart. Is he not a walking mystery like myself?

*Tuesday*

How ashamed am I of myself! Was not what I recorded yesterday a lie? I do like Sennacherib and feel compassion towards him in his present plight; there is no doubt of that. But it was not compassion

43

alone that drove me to visit him yesterday. Rather was it my curiosity to find out something about him.

Watch your pen as you watch your tongue, Pitted Face. Watch your soul against both. And watch yourself against yourself.

### Wednesday

K. P. weeps over his lost money and finds no solace anywhere.

It is now a month since his bank failed, yet he still moves about like a ghost from another world. When forced to speak of that unfortunate circumstance he invariably refers to it as "THE CALAMITY." To him it became an era from which he dates not only the events of his own life but other events as well. "This," he will say, "happened ten years *before* The Calamity;" or that "two weeks *after* The Calamity."

The only calamity is ignorance. The impact of any happening on men may be soft or hard according to whether men know, or do not know, the *real* source and meaning of that happening.

44

## Thursday

I am awake, as witness the palpitations of my heart. Yet my hands do not tremble as on previous occasions.

I have grown accustomed to her visits. To-night I became convinced that her visits were those of a friend and not of an enemy. I saw that in her eyes. The sadness in them, so silent and so deep, seemed to speak compassion and charity rather than resentment and revenge. Because too deep, it appears so awesome, and sends my heart fluttering. It is fluttering yet, although she is gone, and I know that she will not return to-night. Her eyes, however, are still here. They are looking at me. I feel their presence. And their presence frightens and soothes me at the same time.

I stretched myself on the bed for awhile; for I was worn out by too much work. I did not put the light out, fully intending after a short rest and some meditation to write my memoirs.

My mind strayed back into the past endeavoring to find some clews to this riddle called Pitted Face,— who he is, where he was born, and how he came to be what he is and where he is. More than once I had tried that before, but always in vain. Each time I would reach a point in my past which would stand before me like a blind wall; neither my sight, nor my memory could penetrate it. To-night I felt I was almost able to glimpse something behind that wall. But my light went out suddenly, and when I rose to re-light it, I found her standing by my cot . . . And I froze . . .

I did not shake and tremble as on previous occasions. But I felt my heart contract and melt within me; a thick fog enveloped my mind, and I entirely forgot what I was thinking about.

But neither the darkness about me, nor that in my mind was able to hide from my eyes that awful, gaping wound in her throat. Her left hand was still on the wound, the blood gushing from among the fingers. Her right hand was lifted in the air and pointing to the wound. I saw her lips twitch as if whispering some syllables. But I could hear nothing. Perhaps I was too agitated to hear.

She lingered much longer this time than on any of her previous calls. The feeling gripped me very strongly that she was not a stranger to me. I could almost recall where I had met her. More than that, I almost recalled her name. Just then she disappeared as mysteriously as she appeared, leaving me more bewildered than ever.

In vain do I try now to bring back her features. The mist is again thick in my mind.

I know her; I know her. There is no doubt of that. But who is she?

### Friday

Silence.

### Saturday

Silence.

### Sunday

The Battle of Life.

To hear those words, or just to look at them, is to feel crammed, frightened and ill at ease. One would imagine that the whole world was but an endless battlefield where all things and beings were engaged in a stubborn, ferocious, merciless and bloody fight, with no one in command except the dark, unruly passions of each individual fighter. Each against all, and all against all for what each believes to be his right and his due in which others could claim no share. The fighters end where all fighters end,—in death.

It would be more fitting by far to call it The Battle of Death. What has Life to do with it? And when was Life ever a fight?

Life has always been a school and a forge, and never a battlefield. What appears to the ignorant as a battlefield is but the forge through which Life makes all her children pass in order to purge them from the dross of Time and Space and to make them realize what divine metal they are created from.

What the foolish imagine to be a struggle for food, drink and animal pleasure is but Life's way of tearing the veils off the eyes of her lovers that they may come to see clearly all her abiding charms which have nothing in common with the transient pleasures of the belly and the spine.

That which is transient can never last. That which is permanent can never pass. What, then, is permanent in a world so constantly changing? It is Change itself. Shall we say that Life also is subject to change? Nay, it is the only power that causes things to change, while itself remaining unchanged. It is the unchanging constancy in Change. Let the fighters ponder that.

A school and a forge is Life. She teaches and purges all and everything, no matter how near or far, or what its nature may be. Where is the creature that may be said to be out of Life's reach?

How foolish to speak of some men as "isolationists" and of others as "active fighters"! The man who keeps away from the muddy currents of human life, and is therefore called an "isolationist," is often the one who is deeper into the forge of Life, and keener in grasping her lessons and admonitions. It is he who knows the goal and the way, and is fit to be for others a guide and a leader.

Every fighter is blinded by the fight. Shall the blind lead the blind?

A divine school is Life whose business is to turn out divinities. To be graduated from it is to become a god.

### Monday

May God forgive you your rashness, Pitted Face. With your own hand you have made a breach in the wall protecting your solitude. Would you had never made that call on Sennacherib in the hospital.

Why dwell on that? What happened has happened

because it had to happen. Never bemoan or protest any happening; but look for the reason thereof. Accept it in gladness and say to it: "welcome!" So said I yesterday to the messenger who brought me a message from Sennacherib. And what an odd message! —"Write your will."

What does Pitted Face own in this world, Senna-. cherib, that he may will it to others?

He owns a face pitted with smallpox; and that he has willed a long time ago to worms. There are also certain rags upon his body; but neither those rags, nor that body are his. Both were borrowed from the earth, and to the earth must they be returned. Aside from that he "owns" certain flaming yearnings, incessant and persistent, to know himself. To whom shall he will them but to himself?

What, then, does Pitted Face *really* own? Nothing? God forbid. He owns all things: the heavens and all that is in them, and the earth and all on it. For out of everything above and below has he been fashioned, and by everything above and below does he live. How shall he will those things and to whom, when no one is capable of possessing them excepting those who have dispossessed themselves of everything?

And why does Sennacherib wish me to write my will? What matters it to him if I write it or not? Is he perchance a prophet forewarning me of the nearness of my *hour*? Is there an hour for my *hour*?

*Wednesday*

How very strange! Ever since I received Sennacherib's message I can hardly think of anything but
death. It seems to be in every step I make, in every
mouthful of food I swallow, in every breath I take,
and in every thread on my back. I seem to touch it
in everything I touch, and see it and hear it in
everything I see and hear.

Often have I thought of death before. But never
did it seem so real and so close as now. I thought of
it before as an object of study. Now I feel it to be
studying me. It was distant, and now is near. It was
an abstraction; now it is a reality.

Come, Death! Let us talk it out and settle our
accounts.

Death: Behold me, Pitted Face.

P. F.: Who sent you to me?

Death: You called me, and I responded.

P. F. : I called you? . . . Oh, yes, yes, I did call you.
But why did I call you?

Death: Did you not say that we should talk it
out and settle our accounts? This is not the first time
we talk matters out and settle accounts.

P. F.: I do not recall ever having talked to you
before, or settled any accounts with you.

Death: How shall you remember when you are but a fraction of a man as yet? Behold, you called me but a moment ago and forgot that you called me.

P. F.: Fraction of a man? Nay, a complete man am I, even though I be slight of build and with a face like a worm-eaten piece of wood.

Death: I have no business with the complete.

P. F.: What is your business then?

Death: To complete the incomplete.

P. F.: And when all are complete?

Death: Then Death will die. But all shall not be complete at once and in one lump. Therefore shall death live so long as the heavens and the earth are in an unbroken marriage.

P. F.: When shall Pitted Face be complete?

Death: When he shall neither borrow nor lend.

P. F.: Be clear, I pray.

Death: When he shall not live by death.

P. F.: I repeat, Be clear.

Death: (No response).

P. F.: Would that Death would die and leave us incomplete. Or would that we became complete without the aid of Death.

Death: I had thought you different from the rest of men. You now appear to me as one of the herd, wishing that, which if accorded you, would cause you bitter regrets.

P. F.: I do not understand.

Death: For Death to leave you incomplete, would

not that be the opposite of what you really wish? It was but yesterday I heard you wish you knew who you were.

To reach your completion without passing and re-passing through the gates of Death is quite impossible. Perhaps you will grasp my meaning if I ask you to imagine a world where nothing dies. Picture all things growing and multiplying from eternity unto eternity. Would not a single gnat,—not to say a man,—fill up the universe in the end? Should it occur to you to set a limit to the number of things and their growth, wherewith would you feed them? Do you not love Life because it offers you so many things to eat, to drink, to see, to smell and to touch?

Then were it unavoidable for that which eats to be eaten in turn. For the Earth is a loving mother, and Heaven is a tender father. Everything they bring forth they feed with their own flesh and blood, and sustain with their spirit. The flesh feeds the flesh, and the spirit sustains the spirit. Therefore is flesh made to die, since it is in need of food and is needed as food. What feeds on others must perforce be made food for others. Were it not for that, the heaven and the earth should quickly be choked with their own offspring. Whereas the spirit is sustained with the spirit; and because it has no material substance, it fills the heaven and the earth without making them overflow.

Has Pitted Face lived for so long without borrow-

ing and lending? Or does he think that monies and
chattels are the only things capable of being lent
and borrowed? Ideas and emotions, pleasure and pain,
truth and falsehood, all these and kindred values are
being constantly lent and borrowed by men. Let Pitted
Face give back what he has borrowed, and with
interest.

Nor has Pitted Face lived these many years without partaking of the body of the Earth and her offspring. He has stolen the breath of many a living
thing in order to keep his own breath. Now must he
relinquish his breath that other living things may
continue to breathe.

Only when Pitted Face is capable of living without
causing other things to die,—when he becomes a pure
spirit,—will he achieve his completeness and be beyond the reach of Death.

P. F.: Since I was a pure spirit in the beginning,
would it not have been better for me to have so remained forever without being obliged to lend and to
borrow,—to keep my breath by stealing the breath of
others?

Death: It is not for me to answer such a question.
I am but Life's tax collector and the head teacher
in her school. I collect from the living what they have
borrowed from the living. And I teach the living that
everything subject to change cannot be lasting, and
that the lasting cannot be subject to change. So I

fold them and unfold them, time and again, until they learn that lesson to perfection. Once that lesson is perfected, my business is at an end. I consider you one of the bright pupils in my school.

P. F.: What may be your message to-day to Pitted Face?

Death: Behold the message.

Whereupon he handed me a folded piece of paper. When I unfolded it I felt the blood curdle in my veins. My head went swimming, and my tongue became tied. The words I read in that paper were no other but the words in Sennacherib's message: "Write your will." When I regained control of myself I went back to my colloquy with Death.

P. F.: What will do you wish me to write when I do not own a thing to will to any creature?

Death: You have your self; will that.

P. F.: To whom?

Death: To yourself.

P. F.: To will my self to myself? I cannot understand.

Death: Give up your transient self for your abiding self.

P. F.: You wish Pitted Face to efface Pitted Face. Do I understand you right?

Death: I wish Pitted Face to become the power that can efface without being effaced.

P. F.: I have effaced much of myself when I

effaced my name from the records of men; when I put my tongue on a fast, and when I bridled my flesh and blood against many of the pleasures of flesh and blood. What more do you wish me to efface?

Death: Efface that Pitted Face who is still exposed to growth and decay.

P. F.: Will you clarify this mystery to me: Why is Pain concomitant to Death? It is my firm conviction that if you had a lieutenant other than Pain, you should not be so feared and so detested in the world.

Death: How simple of heart and mind you still are, Pitted Face, to attribute to me a power which is not mine. I do not store pain in men; I only uncover the pain they have stored in themselves. Men are always storing pleasure; and it is the nature of pleasure when stored to turn into pain, since it was bought with pain. I have no part whatever in what you and others store. Know that and be careful what you store.

P. F.: What is the wisdom—your wisdom—in visiting some early, and some late; as when you carry away a babe in the cradle, while you dally with that babe's great grandmother or grandfather?

Death: My business is to carry out most faithfully what men decree for or against themselves. Consciously and unconsciously they are in constant intercourse with everything in the world: craving some things, shunning some other things, and consuming many things; loving some men, hating some men, and fighting many men. Thus they invite on themselves the inevitable results of all their cravings and actions, whether they know them or not. But the ever-waking eye of Life sees much more than the veiled human eye can ever see. Do you suppose that each time a child is born a new soul is ushered into the world? All souls are old, Pitted Face; and yours is among the oldest. Even a babe has accounts to settle with Life.

P. F.: You have entertained me well, Death; and I thank you. But you have not yet given me the balance of my account.

Death: Write your will.

P. F.: What if I don't write it?

\* \* \*

Whence this merry purring? Is that you my faithful companion?

Welcome, welcome, my priceless friend. Come, jump to my lap. Come, come; forgiven are all your sins. How glad I am to have you for a companion to-night, and to hear you hum your sweet contentment. Did you not hear what Death said a while ago? —"Whoever delights in the meat of rats must not forget that foxes and jackals delight in his meat."

Cat: Death has misled you. What care I for foxes and for jackals so long as there are mice and rats a-plenty in the world?

P. F.: Don't you hate Death?

Cat: How shall I hate it when it is my instrument of life? Shall I hate myself? Am I not death? Have you forgotten what I did with that rat? Ah! Just to bite into the fat thigh of a fat rat is a gift of death too precious to be valued!

P. F.: Perhaps you like death for others but dislike it for yourself.

Cat: Most certainly. Otherwise I should be an idiot.

P. F.: Then you like death and dislike it at the same time. How strange.

Cat: There is nothing strange in that. For, there are two kinds of death: One that we inflict on others; and one that the others inflict on us,—a death that lives by us, and a death by whom we live. Death, too, is in need of life. Without life death should be strangled to death.

P. F.: Is life in need of death as death is in need of life?

Cat: Of course. Life lives by death as death lives by life. And there be two kinds of life also: A life that we sustain; and a life that sustains us. Ah! Just to be looked at by a coy she-cat burning with passion for the seed of life within me! Is not that a gift of life worth all the treasures of the world?

P. F.: Yours is a tongue much more clever than even that of Death. Tell me please,—what will you do when the hour of your own death strikes?

Cat: I will die.

P. F.: And the pains of death, what will you do with them?

Cat: I will suffer them.

P. F.: And that which awaits you after death,—whether it be continuation, frustration, or annihilation,—do you take no thought of that?

Cat: How foolish to worry about a responsibility which is another's. Death who brought me up and cared for me heretofore is better fitted than I to care for me even after death.

P. F.: Not so with me, my dear companion. It pains me to live by the pains of others, and to have others live by my pain. I would live without paining and being pained. To me Pain is the greatest enemy of all living things.

Cat: It is the greatest friend of all living things.

P. F.: How?

Cat: It makes all living things yearn for a life free of pain; by making them yearn for that life it will help them to attain it.

P. F.: You have spoken my mind. For I have always been longing for a life beyond the reach of pain. Do you think I am like a parched traveler looking for an oasis in a mirage?

Cat: Mirages are often more quenching of thirst than real oases.

P. F.: Perhaps you are right. Yes, perhaps you are right. But have you written your will?

I awakened in the morning with the pen between my fingers, my head resting on the table before me, and the gas jet still burning. Upon my lips were those three words:

WRITE YOUR WILL!

*Wednesday*

K. P. and I are at odds; rather is he at odds with me, and threatens to expel me.

Two nights ago, as I was cleaning the place after all were gone, I found a purse in the toilet-room which must have been dropped by a customer. I put it in my pocket without opening it. Very early in the morning, before K. P. arrived, there was a loud and nervous knock on the door. It was the owner of the purse who had come to ask if, by chance, he had dropped it in the coffee house. I handed it to him at once. Scarcely believing his eyes, he opened the purse, examined its contents and finding them intact, began to shower me with profuse thanks. He even offered me a good sum of money which I refused. Then K. P. walked in, and the man began to tell him of the sleepless night he spent and how he almost lost his wits when he discovered that his purse was lost.

He also told of his fruitless search in many places, of his reporting the matter to the police authorities, and the announcement he placed in many newspapers in the "lost and found" column before it occurred to him to look for the purse in this coffee house where he spent but a very short hour. According to him the purse contained a large diamond ring, a rare pearl and a sum of money,—all worth over $30,000.

Hardly had the owner of the purse crossed the threshold on his way out when K. P. rushed at me, his eyes showing fire, his mouth foaming, and taking me by both shoulders began to shake me violently and to shout:

"You imbecile! You omen of ill luck! You filthy face and clumsy tongue! What earthly good are you? What did you stuff your owlish head with? May you remain without a head. Where did you place your stony heart? May you be left without a heart. Have you so quickly forgotten that I lost all my savings? Have you forgotten that I gave you work, so you could fill your belly and cover up your nakedness? Lost are all my labors on you.

"How do you know that the Almighty in His infinite compassion and justice did not send me this purse as compensation for my lost savings and for the excruciating pains their loss caused me? And who are you to turn back the Almighty's gift? Who are you to shut the door of relief God Himself has

61

opened to me? Are you, the ugliest and the meanest creature of God, more just, perchance, than God?

"Three thousand dollars,—all gone overnight. Yet God,—blessed be His name,—heard my prayers and sent me thirty thousand in their stead; but you,—you idiot,—managed to rob me of the grace of God. How stupid, how stone-blind are you! Did you take pity on the owner of that purse who has more money than he can count, yet you took no pity on me—your master—who has a locust swarm of a family tied to his neck and is barely able to provide them with their daily bread? I swear I shall put you out of here. Yea, I shall put you out."

K. P. raved for a long time. Lost entirely is the new lesson on him. It persists in opening his eyes. He persists in chasing it away.

### Saturday

What a clear-eyed and even-handed judge is Fate! All things and beings in the universe, from the greatest to the least, are weighed every instant in its scales and apportioned their due,—no more, no less. How infinite and accurate is its memory! How acute and impartial its conscience!

62

Each time I think of Fate I bless it and bless Life, its mother; and I say to my mind, "Be quick to learn, and be slow to judge." Would that the judges of men were quick to learn and slow to judge.

**Sunday**

A feeling grips me to-day the like of which I have never experienced before. Perhaps it is Sadness. My heart, my blood, my movements, my breath are all out of tune, as it were. Something clutches them and slows down their rhythm. My ears seem to be tired of hearing, and my eyes of seeing; rather do they seem afraid of hearing and seeing what is not to their liking, or the very opposite of what they like.

In addition to that I feel something resembling regret. But of what?—I do not know. I also feel what may be disquiet and fear; but of what?—I do not know. Parts of me seem to be sliding off the other parts; and everything connected with me, whether near or far, seems to be wearing a veil of a twilight which is neither light nor darkness. Even the pen in my hand is a hesitating pen, devoid of fire and will.

This Sadness has made me think of its opposite,—
of Joy. I do not recall having ever experienced Joy as
men experience it. Is it that till this day I have been
above, or below, Joy and Sorrow? What, then, has happened to me to-day?

Wake up, Pitted Face; wake up! You are deep in
sleep. Have you not found out yet that Joy and Sorrow
are but distractions for the heart? Is there aught in
the world worthy to joy or to sorrow over? Life is
neither Joy nor Sorrow. Life is perpetual serenity.
So be serene.

### Friday

About noon to-day K. P. sent me out on an errand.
The street through which I had to pass, and all the
neighboring streets were so cluttered with humanity
that to cross from one side to the other was practically
a superhuman task. There were as many people on the
roofs and in the windows of the lofty buildings on
both sides as there were on the sidewalks in front of
them. Those on the sidewalks were pressing, jostling
and elbowing each other in an effort to get a foot-
hold in front with the police force using their fists,

and sometimes their clubs, to keep them from overflowing to the pavement in the middle. And what was
the occasion?—The great king of a great land was
visiting the country, and his cortege was to pass
through that section of the city . . .

That was the great occasion which drove those
milling thousands out of their cages into the street
and stopped the countless wheels of their countless
activities in order to give them a passing glimpse of
a royal countenance!

Did it never occur to those people that each of
them was a king, wearing the crown of divinity on
his head, and bearing the fingerprints of Godhood all
over his body, and carrying the surpassing magic of it
in his heart and soul? Was it not more befitting of
them to contemplate night and day their own royal
grandeur instead of rushing out to look at a puppet
king, or at a bloody warrior, or at a clever acrobat?

O Freedom, shut your eyes and turn your face
away from men. Marvel not at their behavior; re-
proach them not for their stupidity; judge them not
according to their ignorance; and cauterize not their
lips each time they speak in vain your holy name.
For their lips do not give utterance to that which is
in their hearts, but to that which they wish had been
in their hearts. What they actually hold and nourish
in their hearts is servitude in its meanest and ugliest
form,—the servitude of man to man. What they wish

65

had been in their hearts is your holy spirit, immaculate, unveiled, beatific and beatifying. Therefore do they glorify you with their tongues, while treading your lovely body with their hob-nailed boots.

I have seen men to-day, O Freedom, crush you under their feet as they shouted madly, "Long live the king!" Rightly interpreted, the cry means: "Long life to Servitude, and death to Freedom." They have not yet come to know that to wish long life to servitude is to wish you death; and to walk in the cortege of servitude is to walk in your funeral.

He who is bought and sold in a slave-market is not a slave. But he is a slave who has made his heart a slave-mart.

Therefore do I keep my peace, while others shout.

### Thursday

Of late I barely recognize myself. Invariably I catch my mind propounding to me the question, "Who are you, Pitted Face?" In vain I try to shut my ears; the question pounds at them with ferocity. To meditate in such circumstances is not only impossible, but something quite painful and akin to insanity. It is

66

now the fourth day that the besetting question stubbornly demands an answer.

And who am I?

I am I. What I know of myself at this very moment
is all I need to know. For the Pitted Face of twenty
years ago, and the Pitted Face of twenty centuries
ago, and the Pitted Face of twenty thousand centuries
ago are all gathered and expressed in the Pitted Face
of this very instant. And the Pitted Face of this instant
is no stranger to me. Whose, then, is the voice that
questions so incessantly, "Who am I?"

Surely it is not the voice of the Pitted Face serving
in a Syrian coffee house in New York, and living a
life of silence and contemplation. It is the voice of
another. I must be two Pitted Faces in one: the first
is a man who has withdrawn from the world of men
and wrapped himself in silence that he may reach a
world of a higher order and move with it in an orbit
other than that of the earth; the second is a man cut
off from the main human current by some human
side-currents, and striving to rejoin the herd. He is
of a lower world and is ill at ease excepting in that
world, with which, so it seems, he has many accounts
to settle.

Hence that furious war raging within me of late.
At times the magnet of the earth and all the earth
passions is so strong upon me that I feel on the point
of plunging headlong into that foaming sea which is

human life. At other times I am drawn up to the regions of pure thought and spirit. Between the two magnets I am a Pitted Face who knows himself, and a Pitted Face who knows not himself, and therefore questions, "Who am I?" I now feel as if the second were about to wake from a long, deep sleep. He would know whence he came, and thither would return.

The outcome of the war is still in the balance. Which Pitted Face will win?

**Sunday**

To-day my known and my unknown selves conversed together. Said my unknown self to my known self:

"Who are you?"

To which my known self responded:

"I am nothing and all things."

Then my unknown self put the question:

"Whence came you and whither are you bound?"

And my known self replied:

"From eternity to eternity."

Whereupon my unknown self was puzzled, and after a pause of silence said:

68

"And who am I?"

Receiving no answer but deep silence, he became much perturbed and repeated his question in evident anger and impatience:

"Tell me who I am; for you know my secrets, and I don't."

My known self kept his peace. Then was my unknown self infuriated, and again he hurled the question threateningly at my known self:

"Tell me who I am; else loose my tongue and let me be, for I am tired of being dumb."

At that point the features of my known self contracted in pain, and he mumbled with infinite sorrow in his voice:

"Give me time, and you shall have your wish."

And he wept.

### *Tuesday*

The whole day passed with my mind hovering about *her*. In vain I tried to switch it to another track. It ran like a wind-blown fire in the dead brush. It was about midnight when I took my pen to write; but the pen would not obey me. I put the light out and tried to surrender to sleep; but sleep refused to imprison me. Suddenly I felt the darkness about me tremble like a black sheet shaken by some hidden hands. Just as suddenly *she* emerged out of the darkness a luminous white shadow, dressed in transparent silk of dazzling whiteness. Softly and gently she approached my cot, her marble-like arms extended forward, the wound in her throat still gaping as before, and the sadness in her lovely eyes as deep, as quiet, as awesome as ever. Added to that sadness was a touch of fear, perplexity, or anxiety.

I was startled, but felt no chills up and down my spine. My heart accelerated its beats, but did not sink down to my soles. My eyes stared, but there was no veil drawn over them. I was capable of fixing them on her face without having them slide, in spite of me, down to the ground. What a lovely face, and how very unlike any other face! It seemed as if fashioned from pure love and pure pain, or as if meant to portray love and pain in eternal marriage.

I asked her: "Who are you? And what seek you of a man with a face like a worm-eaten piece of wood?" How great was my astonishment, nay, my joy, when I noticed her lips twitch as if attempting to articulate something. I listened with every fibre in my body. For a moment as brief as a wink it seemed to me that I heard what resembled a human voice, and what sounded like a word beginning with SH and ending with a B. But it was a very fleeting moment.

70

What happened afterward, I cannot recall. I recall only how she bent over me and touched my forehead with her lips giving me the sensation of having been touched with two live embers. Stung and startled, I jumped to my feet and wished to grasp her; but I found myself grasping darkness. Even at this minute, as I write what I am writing, the perspiration drips from my forehead but does not soothe the burn she left thereon.

Now that she is gone I find I am thinking of love,— the love of man for woman. I imagine myself in love with a woman like this woman, and imagine her in love with me. Then I think of men and women and how almost invariably they lead their love to the altar of marriage there to immolate it and cremate it and to be immolated and cremated by it. Marriage is love's crematory, indeed. While love draws the lovers heavenward, marriage drags them earthward. Love would burn up the lover to project him a shaft of light into space; marriage would grind him and scatter him as dust in the air. Love is a melting, an evaporation, and a diffusion; marriage is a freezing over, a cracking and a splitting.

How does Love, which is a glowing fire, submit to marriage which renders it a heap of cold ashes?

Why dwell on that when, in my case, neither love nor marriage shall ever have a share in my life?

*Thursday*

The Sea!
She attracts me these days as does the mother's breast a suckling babe. I went to her to-night and, intoxicated with her aroma and her deep-throated melodies, began to sing to her incoherent songs.

Sea, spacious sea,—my cradle and the cradle of all Life,

Sea, restless sea,—the heaving, overflowing breasts of the Earth,

Sea, sparkling sea,—the stainless, polished mirror of the Sky,

Sea, roaring sea,—the deep voice of the ages and my voice,

Sea, palpitating sea,—the heart of God and my heart,

Gatherer of the scattered, and scatterer of the gathered,

Bearer of our sins, and washer of our impurities,

Teacher of sublimity and meekness,

Symbol of far-flung ambition and bound-up contentment,

A drop in an infinity, and an infinity in a drop,

Somnambulist ever awake, yet ever asleep,

Dreamer of dreams we dream, and dreams we never dream,

Possessor of the earth, and possessed by the earth,

Your eternity is but a wink, and your wink is an eternity,

And Time is asleep in your bosom the sleep of the just!

· Would that men had eyes capable of seeing the unseeable, and ears so keen as to hear the unhearable. Perhaps, then, they could see you, and hear you, and understand you. Then should they unburden to you their hearts before unburdening their bellies; and should rush to bathe their souls in your purity before bathing their bodies. For joy and sorrow are equally alien to your heart. When sorrow touches your hems it loses its sting and claw. When joy dips in your waters it emerges clean of foolish gaiety and childish self-assertion.

I love you, Sea. I love your peaceful rebellion, and your rebellious peace. For your rebellion and peace are my rebellion and peace. I love your foam and waves. For in me also are waves crested with breaking foam. I love your out-going and your in-coming. For in me also are passions going out and passions coming in. But above all I love your eternal yearning; how like my own yearning it is!

We are two seas, O Sea. But Pitted Face is the broader, the deeper, and the more lasting sea. For a day shall come when you shall contract and finally dry up. Whereas Pitted Face shall not contract except to spread out; and shall not be emptied save to be filled unto eternity.

Yea, two seas are we, my delectable Sea. But Pitted Face is the more lasting of the two.

### Sunday

Sennacherib is back from the hospital with the scars still showing in his face. Although he would not look me straight in the face, I caught him more than once looking at me out of the corner of his eye. I am sincerely pleased to see him back, safe and sound, but would utter no word or make a gesture expressive of that pleasure. I wonder why he shuns and dislikes me so much.

Is it not odd to love a person who hates you? I had always believed Love to be stronger than Hate; that Hate engendered only Hate, as Love engendered Love. Why is my love for Sennacherib unable to beget me anything but hate, and his hate for me unable to beget him my hate?

74

## Friday

Often I marvel at myself when I think that much of what makes others happy does not make me happy, and that which makes them miserable does not make me miserable. Am I not made of the same clay as other men?

There is this coffee house. Small, obscure and insignificant as it is, it seems to represent quite fairly all the cares, the problems, the joys and the sorrows of the earth as daily displayed by our customers.

Here are aired the complex problems of sex from the leaping fire of infatuation to the cold ashes thereof; from the ecstasy of marital union to its endless headaches; from the passion for children to the bitter complaints of the pains and responsibilities they entail. A meeting and a parting; an enchantment and a disenchantment; a mouthful of honey and a cupful of gall; a flow and ebb; a victory and a defeat; a sacrificial deed and a deed for spite; a benediction and a curse; a hopeful prayer and a morbid blasphemy,— all shunning light and breeding in the dark where lowly passions take on the lustre of pure virtue, and where the ashes of those passions appear as gold dust. Hearts budding forth to pleasure are quickly occupied

75

by pain. And flesh clinging to flesh is soon made to rot and to disintegrate. And blood setting fire to another blood, only to turn in the end into deadly pus.

Here, too, are threshed all the problems of trade, of politics, of social and religious intercourse. Producer and consumer; employer and employee; landlord and tenant; prices and rents; profit and loss; taxes and the evasion thereof; good faith and bad; fair dealing and double-dealing; success and failure; prosperity and depression; governors and governed; law-makers and law-breakers; judges and litigants; justice and injustice; lords and plebeians; parties and cliques; revolt and submissiveness; unrest and stagnation; creeds and dogmas; temples and congregations; gods that stone and gods that are stoned; prophets that bind and prophets that split; a here and a hereafter; a heaven and a hell; dying to live and living to die. Bound up with all that are darts poisoned with hate and vindictiveness, and wars whose fires now flare up to the skies, now smolder in the hearts of men and consume them in the end. Lives bud and are nipped in the bud; yet no one seems to ask, "Is it for that we were given life, and the earth was made our home?"

Had I nothing to base my judgment on excepting what I see and hear all about me, I should declare most emphatically that men's life was nothing more than an unbroken chain of problems of which they were impotent to solve the least. Are not their main problems of to-day the same as those of thousands of years ago? As time goes on these problems grow more varied and more complex, with no solution in sight. What is the sense and worth of a life made up of a series of problems which cannot be solved excepting by giving birth to a new one? It would have been far better for a man condemned to such a life if he had never been born.

Yet I, though a man, see no trace of such problems in my life. If there is a problem in my life, it is the problem of knowing myself. And I am confident that He who set this problem for me and lit up this consuming yearning within me for its solution will ultimately lead me to the right answer. That yearning has been my savior so far from the other problems of the world and is the guide that shall lead me to my goal. As it saved me, so it shall save others. Where it leads me, it shall lead them. For Man was born to life, not to death; to knowledge, not to ignorance; to freedom, not to slavery.

But there is a season for each man; and Time is long, long, long.

**Thursday**

Seeker of Perfection! How noble the goal!

What can be nobler for a man than to direct his whole heart and mind towards the aim of breaking the seals of things so as to know them all, to command what now commands him, to lead what now leads him, and to create what he pleases when he pleases? Ah, just to ride Time instead of being ridden by Time; to will and have no opposition to your will; and to speak and feel that the words spoken set a goal and blaze a path to the goal!

Glory, and more glory to you, Seeker of Perfection. And woe, and more woe to them that deride you!

Yet does my heart bleed for you, my friend; aye, my heart bleeds for you; for the road to Perfection is dotted with pitfalls.

A sweet, sparkling eye may lead your eye astray; a honeyed lip may sear your lips with an innocent kiss; a passion-inflamed blood may set your blood on fire. So shall you be swerved from your path, yet shall think yourself pursuing the same path. And so shall you be consumed by your earth passions, yet shall continue to believe that the fire consuming you is no other than the fire of your yearning for Perfection.

While men all around you seethe, and foam, and jealously watch your every step, your every move, and even count your heartbeats, to giggle at your first stumbling and to shout in derision:

"Behold the seeker of Perfection stumble and bite the dust! He had thought it in his power to soar above and beyond us. Look how he has hurtled down from his height and is back as one of us. He had called us slaves to earth passions; now he is bound hand and foot by one of our passions. We counselled him against his rash venture, but he heeded not our counsel. We tried to turn him back, but he stubbornly refused to turn. Did we not say to him that flesh and blood were merciless masters which brooked no disobedience to their orders? But he would not believe what we said. He foolishly imagined himself mightier than flesh and blood. Let him now pay the price of his foolishness."

Nothing is so unpalatable to men as to see one of their own kind break out of their cages and soar away beyond their reach. And nothing gratifies them more than to see that man struck down and forced to crawl back into the cage. Therefore do they turn their lips at seekers of Perfection whenever those seekers make the slightest slip.

Whereas I,—the man so obscure and so insignificant,—each time I hear of a man straining after Perfection I wish I could make of my heart a carpet for his feet, and of my soul a fence for his soul. For the perfection of a single man is a surety for me and for all men of ultimate perfection.

There be four kinds of men:

The man who is mostly beast and partly man. The man who is half beast and half man. The man who is mostly man and partly beast. And the man who is all man.

The first neither thinks of Perfection nor governs his acts thereby. The second dreams of Perfection, but makes no effort to seek it. The third dreams of Perfection, meditates on it, believes in it, yearns for it and seeks it with all the means at his command. The fourth is past the stage of thinking, meditating, yearning and seeking, as well as past the stage of being affected either by hissing or by applause. The third of these is more deserving of love, appreciation and forgiveness, than the rest. For he is called to fight not only the beast in himself, but also the men who are mostly beasts, and the men who are half beasts and half men. It is they who strew his path with snares and help the beast in him against the man, that he may remain forever in their cages and as one of them.

Perfection! How near, yet how distant; how sweet, yet how bitter you are!

Perfection! Count not my transgressions against you.

Perfection! Let my yearning for you be my justification in your eyes.

*Tuesday*

Man—the lord of creation. How most absurd the notion!

The first attribute of a lord is to be a master instead of being mastered; to dictate rather than be dictated to; to order and be obeyed rather than be ordered and obey. Is man—as we know him to-day—anywhere near that lordship?

Had man been the lord of creation, it could not have caused him any harm or any pain of any kind. Yet is he harassed with more pains at the hands of nature than he can keep record of, let alone Death and its countless varieties and causes. From a grain of sand to the farthest sun in the firmament; from a drop of water to the largest ocean; from a gnat to the elephant; from the softest breeze to the maddest cyclone; from the least blade of grass to the mightiest oak,—from all things in nature man is showered incessantly with trials, pains and misfortunes. How, then, has he the temerity to claim lordship over nature?

Furthermore, if man is the lord of nature as he claims to be, he should begin by asserting his lordship over himself, since he is part of nature. He should

81

be able to govern his dreams at night and his thoughts
and actions in the day. It should be easy for him to
cut his whole body—its form, its color, its weight,
its movements and instincts—after a pattern to his
own liking. It should be further possible for him to
rule all his mental, spiritual and physical faculties
in perfect conformity with his thoughts, deeds and
desires. Even sleep, hunger, thirst, sex and other
passions should be more obedient to his will than
is his small finger; nor should hate, anger, vindictiveness, hope and despair have any sway over his heart.

Nay. Man is not yet lord of creation, though he
is destined to become such a lord some day.

Instead of being man's domain, nature to-day is
his mirror. Whatever be the mysteries, the comeliness and uncomeliness, the good and evil man sees
in nature, they are but the reflections of his own
mysteries, his comeliness and uncomeliness, his good
and his evil. As man is, so is nature about him. The
man whose life is beautiful, and whose thoughts are
clean sees nature beautiful and clean. The man whose
life is ugly, and whose mind is unsettled and disturbed
sees nature as ugly, as unsettled and disturbed. The
key to nature is not in nature itself, but in the tiny
pupil of each man's eye. If the soul looking out of
that pupil be an enlightened soul, then all it sees
is light. The key is in the inner light.

Whoever would know nature must first know himself. Whoever would be the lord of nature must first become the lord of his own soul.

*Monday*

And the will,—your will, Pitted Face,—is it not time you wrote it?

Yes, yes. Let us write:

My Pen, so smoothly gliding over this sheet of paper,—what makes you glide?

Is it my fingers? But my fingers are moved by my thoughts. Is it my thoughts? But my thoughts are seeping from that Mind universal whence all thoughts seep and flow. Whatever be the power that moves you, my Pen, may it be blessed.

You have been to me a lip and a tongue, my Pen, and the best of companions as well. Often have you disobeyed me, and I suffered your disobedience in patience. Often have I restrained you, yet you complained not of my restraint. At times you were a lancet in my hand; at others a magic wand, or an urn of balsam, but never the tooth of a viper. With you I plumbed my depths; by you I scaled my heights.

Often I felt you, my Pen, a ligament in my heart,

an artery in my brain, a string in the harp of my soul.
If I rebelled and stormed, you too rebelled and
stormed. If I was calm and at ease, you too were calm
and at ease.

But you are of reed, my Pen, while I am of flesh
and blood. We can hope to divulge no more of ourselves than is possible for flesh and blood to convey
to the reed, and for the reed to a sheet of paper.
Therefore do I will you to Fire. For Fire alone is
capable of revealing Fire.

Forgive and ask no forgiveness.

And you, my Inkwell, drinking so freely of my
blood. You have been more considerate than I of
your precious trust. You dyed my red blood the color
of night so as to hide it from the eyes of the curious
by making it appear as if it were nothing more than
ordinary black ink. You drank me and I drank you,
my Inkwell; yet neither your thirst nor mine was
quenched. How could I quench your thirst while my
own was so great! How could you quench my thirst,
while so thirsty yourself! Therefore do I will you to
the sea. For the sea alone can quench the thirst of
the sea.

Forgive and ask no forgiveness.

And you, my Clothes, which are so many skins
added to my God-given skin. Vast is the difference
between you and the skin God wrapped me in, from

84

the top of my head to the soles of my feet. A piece
of surpassing beauty and marvelous craftsmanship
is that skin,—so perfect in cut and so precise in fitting.
It stretches when necessary, and contracts when con-
tracting is in order. It renews itself by itself, darning
every rip and mending every break. It breathes with
thousands of nostrils and feels with thousands of
tentacles. In it are deserts and oases, as well as forests
and prairies.

It was tiny when I was tiny, growing apace with
my growth. Never were we parted, not even for a
brief wink. In it I came out of my lesser mother's
womb; in it I shall go back into my greater mother's
womb. Between us is an inviolable covenant for life
and death. Glory to Him who spun and wove the
thread. Glory to Him who cut and sewed.

As to you, my Clothes, neither I can tell, nor any
necromancer can, from the plants of what lands, and
the wool of what sheep and lambs you came. Whose
spindle spun the thread, whose loom wove the tissue,
whose hands cut it and sewed it together? Who can
follow all your mysterious peregrinations before you
came to rest upon my back? As I wear you so many
skins over and above my God-given skin, I do not
know whose love or hate, whose curses or benedic-
tions, whose pleasures or pains, whose tears and
smiles I am wearing in reality. Nor do I know even
a part of the infinite secrets that were hid within

your folds by the sun, moon and stars; by the wind and the sea; and by the mist and the dust of the earth.

Furthermore, you are never *just right,* my Clothes,—too ample in places, in others too scant; modest here, brazen there. Besides, you are but so many pieces stitched together not by love, but by the tailor's needle, and in spite of themselves. The threads that hold you together are a little better than gossamer, and are doomed to decay soon or late, as you are doomed. From that ultimate decay no needle or thread can save you. Between you and my body there is a constant war,—now you are too heavy, now you are too light. I put you on during the day to shed you at night. The day shall come when I shall shed you never to put you on again.

Yet have you drunk, my Clothes, much of my body's sweat. Yet have you heard the throbbings of my heart, and listened to the blood coursing in my veins, and borne your share of my burdens, thus becoming a living part of me. Therefore do I will you to Moth; for there is nothing like Moth to blot out blemishes.

Forgive and ask no forgiveness.

And you, my Eye, with which I beheld the effulgent glory of God. You wonder of wonders, and miracle of miracles. Witness of light, yet itself not light. Peephole of the spirit, yet itself no spirit. Bless Him who fashioned you such an incomparable jewel!

Bless your pupil, my Eye, too small to contain a grain of mustard, yet large enough to contain the world. For the heavens with their nebulae, their suns and constellations, their pleiades and shooting stars, all come to slumber under your lashes. The earth with her peaks and canyons, her plains and forests, her rivulets and oceans, and the things that crawl upon its face and things that ride its air, are all encamped behind your lids. The colors of the rainbow with their countless hues dance upon your iris and bathe in your depths.

Bless you because, even at birth, you had been washed with the light of Beauty and dressed with the salve of Ugliness. Yet Beauty did not blind you to Ugliness, nor Ugliness to Beauty; but, as becomes a tender mother, you enfolded both in your love, thus making it possible for them to live in you as inseparable twins. Whereas I, the fool, persist in siding with Beauty against Ugliness; and till this day neither one would surrender or win the fight. How often you have taught me by proverb and by example that the war I wage with Beauty on Ugliness is but a war I wage on myself; that Beauty and Ugliness have lived in peace, and shall continue so to live until the end of time. But I was not wise enough to learn and to

87

understand. Now do I feel as if I am about to learn and to understand.

I have been most unfair to you, my Eye, and most cruel as well. But you never uttered a plaint, or paid me back in my own coin. Shall ignorance ever be fair, and understanding ever be cruel? Many times you fell on sights so gruesome and so horrid that I wished I were without sight. Many times you caught me views that made me wish I had a thousand eyes. In either case you were entirely blameless and I alone to blame. For I should know that everything partaking of light and life is but a rung in the ladder leading to the heart of light and life, whether we call it Ugliness or Beauty, or whether we brand it as good or as evil. I wish that those who claim that there is but one way and but one door to Truth would take a lesson from you, my Eye. For you have not wended your way into the world of visual things through this thing or that, but through all the things you could encompass. You did not enter the vegetable kingdom through the cedar alone, but through the bramble as well; nor did you enter the animal kingdom through the eagle and the deer, but through the earthworm and the skunk as well. Everything you fell on in the world, whatever its nature, was your door into the universe.

How many roads you made me walk, my Eye; yet till this day I have not reached the end of one. Each road seems as long as Time itself; it would finish us before we could finish it.

88

How many doors you have led me to, my Eye; yet we did not cross the threshold of one. From the grain of sand and the drop of dew to the sun in its orbit and the ocean in its shores,—what an infinite succession of charmed and charming doors! Even now I knock at them with my heart, not with my hand. I cannot tell if my heart will be able to melt them away before they melt it away; or if it will be able to hear their hinges squeak before they hear it squeak.

Other eyes now bathe in tears, now light up with smiles. I do not remember having once moistened your lashes, my Eye, with the salt of a tear, or tickled your lids with the spark of a smile. Odd, indeed, is your lot among the lots of eyes.

Never did I strike in you the fire of any passion, my Eye,—neither the passion of Adam for Eve, nor the passion of the indigent for riches, nor that of the lowly for power, nor of the downtrodden for vengeance. We have lived the years allotted us so far in peace and quiet. But soon we must part; since every lifetime must have an end. And I am writing my will. To what, or to whom, should I will you, my Eye?

I will you with the countless worlds you contain, and with the shadows of dreams indescribable ever flitting in the shade of your lashes; aye, I will you with all your wonders to Worms.

Yes, to Worms—Worms—Worms!

Forgive and ask no forgiveness.

And you, my Ear, that helped me to hear the conscience of all things by helping me to hear my own conscience,—you, too, are a marvelous tool. You transmit to me all that transpires within the inner man from his birth to his death. You also transmit to me everything that the birds, the insects, the beasts, the trees, the grasses, the waters, the winds and the thunders say in their many moods and tongues, and in their various habitats. Whether or not I understand what they say,—with that you have no concern. For you are but a messenger; and a messenger's business is to deliver the message faithfully. And you are a most faithful messenger.

Pity you, my Ear, for you have known no rest since you and I came to be. Night and day do you receive and deliver messages. In one short minute you may bring me a thousand communications. But I am awkward and slow to read. Out of a thousand messages you bring me I may not read more than one,—and even that I may comprehend conversely; yet will I behave as if I had rightly read and understood the thousand. Unmindful of all that, you pursue your labors without a halt, a murmur, or a plaint. All manner of sounds, soft and rough, high and low, pleasant and unpleasant, rush into you from every side and at every moment without ever causing you to overflow, to be clogged, or to shut your gates in disgust.

Were it possible for me, my Ear, to press together all the sounds that found their way into you during the last three decades, then to make of them a kind of sound-bomb, then to explode that bomb in the air,—do you not suppose that the repercussions thereof would whip the oceans into fury, and make the mountains click together like the teeth of one in the chills of malaria? Would it not concuss every brain in every skull, break every drum in every ear, and throw the air into fits of convulsions?

Were it also possible for me to retrieve every word you heard since you began to hear, and to put those words on paper, then to spread out those papers over the earth,—do you not estimate that they would cover the earth?

Words—words—words! Hornet words and wasp words; scorpion and adder words; swine and fox words; whale and minnow words; ant and beetle words; cockle-burr and briar words; bog and sewage words; fire and ice words; spear and dagger words; lead and powder words; snail and octopus words; anvil and hammer words; drum and fife words; thief and robber words; raven and vulture words; peacock and sparrow words,—what an endless scroll! What a shameful scroll!

To be fair, however, one must add to that scroll a pinch of sweeter and brighter words such as those of justice, faith, freedom, fidelity, nobility, truth, love, purity and beauty, even though they appear in it as out of place and very ill at ease. Aye, what a scroll, what a jungle, what a madhouse! No mind, however strong, can feel in it at home. No imagination, however keen, can wade through its morass. Yet you, my Ear, so tiny and so stark, are able to contain it all. Truly you are a wondrous apparatus and a spacious storehouse.

More wondrous yet than you, my Ear, is Pitted Face who is able to hear all that you hear and something else besides. And Pitted Face is now writing his will. To whom or to what shall he will you?

To Worms—Worms—Worms!

Forgive and ask no forgiveness.

And you, the bones, the skin, the hair, the muscles, the joints and the entrails of Pitted Face; you, his hands and his feet, his tongue and his lips, his teeth and his nails, his blood and his brain,—I do not know, in truth, which of you is the most marvelous and most important in the structure of the life which is my life. And how shall I know being the structure and the dweller therein?

Surpassing in conception and grandeur of execution is that structure. Everything in it is ever a-stir, knowing neither idleness nor rest. Surpassing also in wonder is the dweller therein who, while occupying all of it, lives and behaves as one occupying but a small corner thereof. When busy with hands, or feet, or mind he pays no heed to the rest as if it were not his. Whereas that of which he may be unmindful at any given moment is always mindful of him and carries on in good faith the work appointed it for its lord's comfort. Not a hair, nor a nail, nor a blood molecule but performs its task night and day; and the tasks of all are so masterfully co-ordinated as to merge into one master-task which is the task of the living body.

Who can give an accounting, my body, of all the steps we walked and the distances we travelled? Who can make a list of all the things we consumed from the larders of the earth and the sky, and all that the earth and sky consumed of us? Who can count the breaths you borrowed from the air and the breaths you gave back to the air? Could we but gather those breaths together, my Body, what storms and whirlwinds should we be able to unleash! Ours, however, is the task not to unleash, but rather to leash the storms and the whirlwinds and to render them as languid breezes.

Behold, My Body; I am now writing my will. To whom, or to what should I will you?

To Worms—Worms—Worms!

Forgive and ask no forgiveness.


And you, my Heart!

Heart—Heart . . .

Heart—Heart—Heart . . .

Pulse of the Unseen in the seen,
Chronometer of the chorus of the spheres,
Cradle of hours, centuries and eons,
Vessel of joy and sorrow,
Fountainhead of light and darkness,
Incubator of care and pain,
Nuptial couch of life and death,
Altar of yearning, and pulpit of hope,
Pasture of dreams, and wilderness of delusions,
Quiver of doubt, and shield of faith,
Guide of the blind and the seeing,
Meltingpot of yesterday, to-day and to-morrow,
Urn of charity, and spout of vengeance,
Vineyard of peace and winepress of war,
Space illimitable in prosperity, and a needle's eye
in time of hardship,
Holy book written with blood on sheets of blood,
Bower of God, and cesspool of Satan,
Harp choking with its own melodies,
Hunger unappeasable, and thirst unquenchable,
Dwarf laying low the giants, and giant mauled
by dwarfs,
Devout, whose prayers are blasphemies,
Blasphemer, whose blasphemies are devotions,
Recluse within the breast of a recluse,
Heart—Heart—Heart,
Heart—Heart . . .
Heart . . .

94

To Worms—Worms—Worms!

.. .. .. .. .. .. .. .. ..

You have bought your pains with your sins,
Forgiven are your sins,
And blessed be the pains.

### Tuesday

It was good that you wrote your will, Pitted Face;
for it made you realize how infinitely rich you were.
You believed all along that you were destitute; now
you have come to know that all the far-flung worlds
throb, and live and move within the small world
which is you.

Had you a particle of envy, you should be envious
of yourself. But envy is alien to your nature, and your
riches are far beyond computing. Were you to live
as long as a thousand Methuselahs, you would barely
exhaust a trifling fraction thereof. Shall we say that
He who gave you so much was too lavish in giving, or
was too rash and short-sighted in that He struck no
fair balance between His gifts and your needs? It
ill behooves you, Pitted Face, so to think and speak.

Say rather that you are rash and short of sight

95

in thinking that He who bestowed on you all these glorious worlds allotted you no more than three decades in which to uncover their charms and to enjoy them, body and soul. How do you know that in giving you so much He did not give you an eternity in which to know the full value of the gift? How do you know that the sleep of death is not another kind of sleep from which you shall wake up unto another day?

Be of good cheer, Pitted Face. The will you wrote this side of the grave shall one day appear to you a thing of mock and shame the other side thereof. The sleep of death shall whet your appetite for fuller enjoyment of life, and you shall wake from it with keener hunger for more life, as you wake from your nightly sleep to meet with a renewed vigor the challenge of a new day.

*Friday*

Were all the secrets of the universe to be revealed to you, Pitted Face, save the secret of Creative Will, you should still be a straw in a gust of mad wind, or a guideless blind man in the bowels of a blind night.

96

*Saturday*

Take it, Pitted Face! Take a lofty message from a noble messenger, and an eloquent lesson from a most capable teacher.

Too far have you gone in your self-deceit. So much so that you have come to consider yourself as almost free of fault and clean of all impurities that harbor decay. You have even come to believe yourself a friend of Fate, well buttressed against all pain. Lo! A tooth,—a mere tooth,—has now come to rob you of the joy of eating, sleeping and meditating, from the rising of the sun to the setting thereof, and from the setting thereof to the next rising. Not contented with that, it distorts your already distorted face by swelling one cheek away out of proportion to the other, and by making the swelling spread up to your eye till it is almost shut.

A tooth, a mere tooth, rebelled against you and, lo ! Your thoughts are scattered, your nerves are wrecked, your dreams are driven helter-skelter, your patience is dried up, your will is paralyzed, your pride is humbled, and you are made to center all your mind upon that tooth as if it were the alpha and

the omega, the center and the circumference of your
life. A tiny piece of bone in your jaw assumes the pro-
portions of a monster serpent with a thousand jaws and
teeth sucking your brain, gnawing away your sinews,
breathing poison into your blood, and clutching your
heart as with a vise, with no help in sight but the
dentist's forceps!

How pathetic and ridiculous to appeal for succor
from a tooth for one whose mind would belt the heavens and the earth; whose imagination roams eternities,
and whose marvelous body is made up of countless
wonders, the least of them being two rows of teeth in
two jaws!

Is it not to marvel at that he who trains the wild
beasts; who crumples mountains, rides the storm,
subdues the deeps, and forces lightning to be as one
of his servants should be so helpless in his fight with
a rebellious tooth, and should suffer at its hands such
excruciating pains?

Think of this, Pitted Face: How come that a tooth,
so helpful heretofore in the building of your body, so
friendly and so benign, should suddenly shift from
the camp of builders to that of demolishers, and thus
be turned into a deadly foe? Have you the least doubt
that you must have maltreated it sometime, somehow?
But your memory is far too wayward and short. You
do not recall how, when, and where you were
negligent of your tooth and deaf to its appeals. There-

fore did it strike back with so many shafts of pain
that you may learn what you have not learned:
namely, that you, yourself, consciously and unconsciously, are the author of your own pain of which
the fates are but witnesses.

Where is your creative will, Pitted Face? Why do
you not call upon it to switch your mind off your
pain, to stay the march of decay in your tooth, and
to order that tooth to become once more a faithful
and a diligent builder in your body?

Know, Pitted Face, that between you and the
knowledge you seek stretch many jungles and deserts
every foot of which is crisscrossed with puzzles and
pains, so long as you cannot command your body as
you will. If you had that knowledge, you would not
eat or drink, purpose or do, imagine or desire anything likely to bring decay to your tooth and ache to
your head, or to cause the slightest disturbance in
the perfect balance prevailing among all the organs
and parts of your body.

But you are still far from that knowledge, Pitted
Face; yea, very far. To yearn for it with a burning
passion, though quite commendable, is not enough to
shield you from pain. Neither is it enough to meditate, to bridle the tongue, to put the flesh on fast,
and to train the heart to be chaste, contented and
tolerant. All that may mitigate pain, but is not that
impregnable wall which pain cannot break through.

That wall is Knowledge. Where there is ignorance, Pitted Face, there is pain. Where there is pain, there is the challenge to storm the citadels of ignorance and to ransack its dens. Therefore is pain such a priceless guide and such a splendid teacher, but to those only who have eyes to see and hearts to learn.

You ask, Pitted Face,—and very properly, "What good are the lessons given me by Pain after the mischief is done,—after the tooth is gone?"

And Pain would answer you, "A lesson you do not apply to-day, may be applied to-morrow. Nothing learned is ever lost; and the time to learn is all of time."

You ask again,—and also very properly,—"If pain be of benefit to the pained, what are the benefits of pain to one on his death-bed? Will he profit by pain even in the grave?"

And Pain responds, "Therein is the greatest lesson for those who are keen enough to learn. Pain is a tree whose fruit is knowledge. And knowledge is the food wherewith a wise traveler provides himself from one stopping place to the next.

"A wise and forceful instructor is Pain in everything it teaches men between the cradle and the grave. Do you suppose that it loses its force and wisdom, and falls into dotage so soon as men reach the end of their tether, and goes on instructing them to no purpose at all?

"A sweet and sustaining food is knowledge

extracted from pain. Do you allow that Life who was tender and loving in providing the traveler with wholesome food from the start of his journey would suddenly become so hard of heart and so senile as to load him at his death-bed with provisions which he can put to no use at all after death?

"How do you know, Pitted Face, that a dying person is not on a pilgrimage, and that his pains this side of the grave are not his food for a journey the other side of the grave? If it were otherwise, your life and all life would be a travesty,—a thing devoid of purpose and of meaning. For what could be the meaning of a life entirely effaced by death?"

Again you ask, Pitted Face, and again very properly, "Shall we say, then, let pain be ever welcome?"

"Nay!" shall be the answer. "Rather should you say, 'Away with Pain!' For its face is not a comely face, and its touch is not a pleasant touch."

Is Pain, then, your friend and foe at the same time, Pitted Face?

Aye, it is even so. You have not befriended him except to fight him, and you have not fed him save to starve him in the end. Would that men could forget all their enmities excepting their enmity to Pain; and put an end to every war except their war on Pain. Which is to say, would that they learned well the lessons taught them by Pain so as to vanquish Pain with knowledge.

But men are blind. They would fight Fate which

is of their own making, and let Pain have sway over their lives. The dupes!

## Wednesday

Pray, Pitted Face; pray hard. This turmoil in your head and heart will not be stilled except by prayer.

Whence is this turmoil, Pitted Face, which makes you feel as if your head and heart were not your head and heart? Will you allow a passing phantom to play havoc with your equipoise, to take possession of your heart and mind, to subjugate your will and leave you prostrate, submissive and devoutly awed?

But it was a phantom unlike other phantoms,— the phantom of a maiden cloaked in crimson whose every thread streamed with breath-taking, virgin femininity which, as by charm, set my body on fire. I felt its intoxicating warmth creep in every corpuscle of my blood, in my skin and bone, in the lids and lashes of my eyes, and in every muscle of my body. The feeling soon became one of waves tossing me right and left, and ended by submerging me from head to foot. Anon I became a flaming torch. A mad passion seized me to burn the maiden and myself in the selfsame fire, in the selfsame forge and to live with her an eternity in a wink.

The stature was *her* stature; so were the face, the hair, the breasts, the hands; and so was the neck, this time marble-like and with no trace of blood and of an awesome, gaping wound. The eyes, too, were her eyes; but that deep sadness in them was veiled with a veil too subtle for words, too elusive to paint; it gave forth the fragrance of maturing femininity just out of the bud,—a fragrance so tantalizing, so inebriating, so irresistible.

I do not recall how she stepped out of the night, how she touched me and set me on fire. Nor do I recall what I said to her and what she said to me; nor what power dragged me down to the ground and made me kneel at her feet. All I recollect is that she passed her delicate hand over my eyes and unfolded before me a small piece of paper on which were written the following words:

*"I slew my love with my own hand, for it was more than my body could feed, and less than my soul hungered after."*

Immediately after, she was swallowed up by night.

Night, compassionate night! Why did you not swallow me with her? I am no longer myself.

Pray, Pitted Face, pray.

**103**

*Thursday*

K. P. has a new care to-day. It is the marriage of
one of his daughters,—the third of four sisters two of
whom are old maids with no hope of ever marrying.
Unwilling to accept the lot of her older sisters, the
third daughter decided to grasp the first proffer of marriage made to her no matter by whom. This proffer
came from a widower twenty years her senior, and the
father of a boy and two girls, all married long ago.
Rheumatic and dropsical, he is practically unfit to do
any work. His only claim to the rights of marriage is his
being a male and, as such, fit to be stamped a "husband" by men's social and religious codes.

That was revealed to me this morning by K. P.
in a friendly tête-à-tête. Said he unexpectedly:

"Fie on you, Pitted Face! Fie also on these topsy-
turvy times in which the children have become so
willful and so brazen as to manage their lives in their
own ways, quite independently of their parents. There
is one of my own daughters. She is on the point of
marrying a man of whom we know nothing. Do you
think she consulted us in the matter? Not at all. She
simply announced to us her decision with an air of
finality,—that's that. When we found out that the

104

man was a widower and fit for nothing we tried to
dissuade her. The result was that she dubbed us old-
fashioned, ignorant and barbaric, and turning her
upper lip in scorn, went on with her preparations
for the wedding. What is more provoking, she feels no
scruples in asking her mother and me for money.
What say you to that?"

Receiving no answer from me, he went on:

"Fie on you. One can hope for no help from
you,—not even for counsel. Neither in peace nor in
war; neither in hard nor in easy times are you of any
service. Had you not been dumb, I would not mind
having you for a son-in-law in spite of your pitted face.
But you are dumb." And after a pause of reflection,
"A dumb bachelor is perhaps better than a speaking
widower and an old cripple. Would you take my
daughter for wife if she agreed to take you for her
husband?"

*    *    *

Pray, Pitted Face; pray for K. P., and what man
is not K. P. insofar as marriage and other social insti-
tutions, traditions and conventions are concerned?

Many a book has swallowed up its author. Many
a creature has vanquished its creator.

So it is with men. The codes, the rituals and the
conventions they have created for their comfort are
now become their masters, and they, the slaves. But
they know it not.

**105**

**Sunday**

A whole week passed and Sennacherib has not been seen in this place. For no apparent or logical reason his absence gave me much concern. The man is not my relative, nor my friend. On the contrary; he returns not even an iota of the good sentiments I hold for him in my heart. More than that; he shuns me and seems to detest me. Why should his absence cause me so much anxiety? What added to my anxiety was the conversation I overheard two days ago between two of our customers. Said one of them:

"Why has Sennacherib stopped coming to this house after he was such a constant attendant, never missing an evening of poker? Do you suppose he is bankrupt? For I rarely saw him win in any game."

To which the other replied:

"Sennacherib bankrupt? Perhaps foxes would become bankrupt of fleas, and meadows of grasshoppers before Sennacherib would lose all his money. Let not appearances deceive you. He is one of the really wealthy. But for a reason which neither I nor anyone can understand he pretends poverty. He *is* a mystery; perhaps a bundle of mysteries."

106

The first: "If what you say is true, he should not be living in a shabby room in one of the shabbiest sections of the city."

The second: "It is as I tell you. Didn't you know that he bought an elegant car?"

The first: "What need has he of any kind of car when he has neither business nor family, and cares next to nothing for trips and merryments? Besides, the clothes he wears are hardly fit for a driver, let alone the owner of a sumptuous car."

The second: "I told you that the man was a mystery. Do you know why he chose for a haunt this very coffee house which is the least of our coffee houses?"

The first: "Why?"

The second: "Because Pitted Face is here."

The first: "But what has Pitted Face to do in the matter?"

The second: "That too is a mystery. Sennacherib once told me that he had a peculiar pleasure in studying people, particularly those of a queer character like Pitted Face."

The first: "But he seems to dislike Pitted Face."

The second: "On the contrary; he admires Pitted Face and is fond of him, but pretends to dislike him so that Pitted Face would not be aware that he was studying him."

The first: "Very strange."

The second: "Strange, indeed. The world is full of strange things and persons."

The first: "Why did Sennacherib stop coming here? Do you know?"

The second: "I don't. Perhaps he is breaking in his new car. Perhaps he had an accident. Perhaps he left for some unknown destination never to come back again. If he is safe and sound, and still in this city, we shall undoubtedly see him soon."

---

And so it was. Sennacherib came this afternoon and remained till midnight.

I happened to be standing near the door when a luxurious limousine rolled up to the curb. At the steering wheel was Sennacherib himself. When he descended from the car and walked in, his appearance was a matter of astonishment as much to K. P. as to myself. He had on a grey suit of an exquisite texture and very expensively tailored. In his left hand, gloved in white, he held the glove of the right. His hair, lustrous and dark, was carefully combed back. His face looked radiant and freshly massaged. From him was wafted on me a most delicate scent. The moment I inhaled of it I became almost dizzy and felt as if the coffee house had suddenly been transformed into a stately palace each door of which, each window and piece of furniture and tapestry were familiar to me.

More puzzling was the sensation that gripped me at seeing Sennacherib in his new make-up and new car. I had the distinct feeling of having known him long ago. He appeared as being closer to me than is my shirt to my body. To recollect, however, how, when and where I had known him was quite defying to my memory.

No, I do not remember. Yet that delicate, teasing perfume emanating from Sennacherib's clothes made me almost remember. Even now, two hours after he and the rest of the customers left the place, that fragrance seems to tickle my nostrils and play havoc with my thoughts. Now it brings me near; now it tosses me leagues and leagues away, much like a word lost in the folds of memory: we feel it on the tip of the tongue; we almost visualize its letters and hear its footfalls in the ear; yet does it defy our efforts to string its letters into syllables, and to reproduce its footfalls in the ear. At last, tired and numbed, we give up the search. Just then, and without any effort on our part, it floats out of the depths of memory.

Perhaps that perfume, so elusive and so tantalizing, will ultimately unlock the door behind which it is now hiding in my memory. Perhaps that door shall lead me to many other doors. For some reason I am beginning to feel that in my head are many, many doors now securely locked, but on the verge of opening.

Another strange, but very significant incident took

109

place tonight. A few moments before he and the rest of the customers left the place about midnight Sennacherib, without the slightest warning, walked into my "cloister" behind the wooden partition. I was sitting at my desk, my head between my hands, and my mind straining to break through the dark curtains in my memory. Saying nothing at all, and paying no heed whatsoever to my presence, he began to look about the room as one taking measurements, or one studying exhibits in a museum. A moment later he walked out as he walked in,—silent and enigmatic.

You were not impatient in the past, Pitted Face. Be not impatient now.

### Monday

It became clear to me today why Sennacherib visited my cloister last night. Early this morning I found a white, folded paper behind my door. I picked it up and unfolded it, and what did I read in it? This was what I read:

*"I slew my love with my own hand, for it was more than my body could feed and less than my soul hungered after."*

110

God! God of the deaf and dumb and blind! God of recluses and enigmas! What enigma is this? But a few nights ago *she* brought me those same words written in the same hand on the very same paper as Sennacherib brought me last night. To make the puzzle more puzzling the handwriting appears to be almost a copy of mine.

My head is about to split. Is it possible that my fancy is playing tricks with me?

Collect your wits, Pitted Face. It is not your fancy that is playing tricks on you; it is some shadows of your past that are now advancing on you from their dark retreats, and at your own invitation. There must be something in your life that calls them forth at this very juncture of your life; your need for them must be pressing; otherwise they should have tarried longer in their retreats.

Did it occur to you to ask why this paper came to you and to no one else? Can you not see that it came to you because you drew it to yourself? Accept it thankfully, and scrutinize it carefully. Should its meaning be obscure to you today, the morrow is certain to reveal it.

Collect your wits, Pitted Face. Be steady and patient. Let days and nights be delivered of their burdens,—each in its appointed time. You can neither quicken nor retard their deliverance. Sufficient wages for today are the labors of today.

**111**

*Monday*

Today is Labor Day,—a big holiday. Pitted Face is a laborer; but the holiday is not his.

What day is your holiday, Pitted Face? You alone, of all the people of the earth, have no holiday. Nay, you alone have each day a holiday. Does not each day bring you new treasures of thoughts, emotions, and blessings inexhaustible! To enjoy in full but one of those countless blessings, is not that a holiday too wondrous for words? Where is the soul so spacious, so deep and so hungry as to absorb all the blessings of being in one day, or in one year, or in one lifetime, or a thousand lifetimes? Too numerous, too varied and too precious are those blessings for any eye, ear, nose, pocket, or belly to contain them.

Yet men's holidays are feasts for the belly, the pocket, the nose, the ear, and the eye. In their mad rush for stupefying pleasures men become entirely oblivious of the particular blessings on which a given holiday is supposed to focus their minds, be that blessing the birth or death of a prophet, the martyrdom of a saviour, or the blessing of labor and all that labor is able to create.

From early morning till away past midnight this

112

small coffee house was crowded with visitors. K. P.'s pocket waxed fatter and fatter; his eyes grew brighter and brighter; his tongue incessantly smote his teeth and the roof of his mouth. It was his holiday; or rather the holiday of his eye, ear and pocket. As to the blessing of Creative Labor of which this day is supposed to be a reminder, neither he nor any of his customers remembered it with even a passing word. On the contrary; everything he said and did, and everything they said and did was a negation of that blessing and a mockery thereof. They were too busy suffocating their souls to give any thought to life; too absorbed in tearing and effacing to meditate on the glory of Creative Labor.

Ah, blessing of the plow, and pick, and scythe,
Blessing of the forge, and hammer, and anvil,
Blessing of the ax, the chisel and the saw,
Blessing of the spindle, the thread and the loom,
Blessing of the ax-hammer, the plumb and the angle,
Blessing of the paper, the ink, and the pen,
Blessing that sends ships sailing the oceans and the space,
Blessing that bridles lightning and makes it a steed for the mind and a light for the eye,
Ah, blessing of Creative Labor,—the greatest of all the blessings: Forgive men and the ignorance of men. Forgive them all,—the worker and the idler, the dili-

113

gent and the indolent, the optimist and the pessimist, the believer and the unbeliever, the spendthrift and the miser. Forgive even those of them who consider themselves too high, too noble, too supermanic to stoop down to any kind of labor. Forgive them all; for till today they do not know what a divine blessing you are.

Often have I heard men say: "Would we were like the plants of the field and the birds of the air; or like the beasts in the wilds and fishes in the sea." What a disgrace! Having been endowed with the blessings of Creative Labor, do they wish that they were disendowed? Do they not yet know that to create by labor is man's exclusive attribute and the greatest of all gifts wherewith he has been blessed? For through Creative Labor man can hope to reach the throne of God,—to pass from being a creature with limited capacities to being a Creator with unlimited powers to create.

Do they not yet know that Creative Labor is the link connecting man with man, and connecting all men with the rest of creation? Do they not know that it is the crucible wherein all men are made as one man? Truly is mankind but a single man,—the ever-ascending Man,—by virtue of the blessing of Creative Labor.

Here am I,—Pitted Face,—the obscure man wrapped in silence and working in an obscure coffee house in the twentieth century Babel; if I wished to compensate all those that labor for me throughout the world, I should be at a loss to know where to start and where to stop; whom to compensate and wherewith to compensate them.

Wherewith shall I reward those who have sown and harvested that I might be fed; and those who have spun and woven that I might be clothed; and those who have rolled back the darkness that I might have light; and those who have sent forth ships and carriages that I might move from place to place; and those who have invented the letters and the printing-press that I might read and write? How very foolish of me to count all those who worked and are now working for me! They are countless. It is the height of folly then, Pitted Face, for you to say that your soul and body are yours alone; since Creative Labor has mixed in one crucible your flesh and blood with all men's flesh and blood, and your thoughts and emotions with their thoughts and emotions. Your tongue, therefore, is not yours alone; nor is your eye your eye alone. They are everybody's tongue and eye.

Men and women toilers of the world,
You, who entomb their days and dreams in the bowels of the earth,
Who scatter their smiles and tears on the cross-roads of life,

Who suckle their hopes with the blood of their
hearts,

Who feed with their sinews the rocks and brambles
of the wilds,

Who sow their yearnings in inkpots and rainbows,

Who spread their lives over waves and dunes,

Who imprison themselves in cages of banks and
factories,

Who bury their eyes and their ears in ponderous
ledgers,

Who melt away their brains in columns of black
and red numerals,

Whose songs are the whir of wheels and the roar
of avaricious passions,

Whose dance is the dance of the Penny and the
Pound,

You laborers, old and young, male and female,—
whatever be your tint and the work you are called on
to do,—here is an insignificant laborer in an insignificant coffee house stretching forth his hand to you,
and with an open heart blessing you and the labor
you do; for he knows the significance of Labor.

And what is the significance of Labor?

It is the power to knit all lifetimes into one continued lifetime, and to merge all hopes and purposes
into a single hope and purpose, and to direct them all
towards a common goal. There can be no break in
creative human labor until Man achieves that mastery

of himself and the world which alone shall enable him to chart and to create worlds at his own will and pleasure.

Who is so stupid as to set a price, whether in monies or in chattels, on that immeasurable, up-moving pyramid of human labor whose foundations were laid down since Man came into being? Truly it is above and beyond any pricing. A labor that is priceless in its aggregate form is priceless also in its smallest detail. And what man's life-labors are not a detail,—a stone,—in the immense structure of combined human labor? Who, then, is so omniscient as to set a value on this or that man's labor?

But men,—how I pity them!—are ever at pains gradating human labor and setting a price on each grade, the prices varying as much as from a zero to a million. When life which would not be confined and hemmed in any tables, equations, or numbers sets at naught their meticulously and painstakingly worked-out schemes of value, then they squirm and rub their hands in utter despondence; else they seethe, and foam and run over, unleashing their basest and beastliest passions. Instead of working as one team in the rearing up of the glorious pyramid of creative human effort they split into many factions, each hostile to the other and each working for the utter destruction of the other. The sickle becomes a sword; the pickax, a rifle; the pen, a cannon; the ink, gunpowder; and words, bullets and bombs. Thus they tear down today what they built yesterday; thus they turn light into darkness, and the fire of life they quench with the breath of death.

Were mankind to put in my hands the reins of their affairs, I should draft them all into a single army to be drilled and disciplined as the best armies are drilled and disciplined, and to be equipped with all the tools and instruments man has so far invented to make his life tolerable. I should then declare war on the earth to make it give up its treasures; to make accessible its most inaccessible corners; to subdue its haughtiest peaks and its fiercest wilds and jungles; to clothe with verdure its rocks and deserts; to dot its face with peaceful settlements; to blot out all boundary lines from its surface, and to make it a warm, roomy and comfortable home for man. Then would I say to men, "Behold! The earth is yours. Eat and drink heartily of the fruits of your labor. Sing, dance, and play to your heart's content. Yours are the spoils; but yours also is the burden of profiting thereby, and you share equally in both. So long as you are warriors under the banner of Creative Labor, let no one take thought as to what he shall eat, and drink, and wear, and wherein he shall dwell. For all that shall be amply provided you by your own Creative Labor, and by the loving hearts of the earth and sky."

Why, in truth, should not all men be conscripts in

the Army of Creative Labor, fighting each for the other instead of fighting each the other? Why should not their years of service, and their hours of daily work be lengthened or shortened as necessity may dictate? Why should not schools, hospitals, museums, sanatoria, musical bands and orchestras and all the other healthful distractions follow the workers under the command of Creative Labor wherever they may chance to be and whatever be their labor?

When all men's hearts, and minds, and hands are set on conquering the earth to make it yield its goods; and when those goods are distributed among the laborers in as fair a manner as are rations among soldiers, what cause shall there remain for sordid competition, for envy, greed and mad self-extermination? But men are not yet of age. Like irresponsible and foolish children they would rather fight over an apple in the tree than think of ways and means of plucking that apple first, then dividing it as equitably as possible among all.

Ah! Blessing of Creative Labor,—the greatest of all the blessings! Forgive Pitted Face. Forgive all men, and make us worthy of your incalculable bounties.

*Thursday*

What was that ecstasy I felt tonight, and how shall I describe it? It was indescribable. How I wish I had never come out of it.

What made me so ecstatic,—I do not know.

It descended on me all of a sudden and filled me with wondrous light as would the rays of the sun fill a ball of crystal. I felt I was an ethereal being saturated with light and warmth. No longer was I a creature of flesh and blood, and a prisoner of time and space. In fact I was no longer my old self. Everything in the universe, the visible and the invisible, seemed to have melted in me, and I in it. The sun and moon and stars became of me, and I of them; likewise the earth and all the miracles within it, upon it and around it.

All seemed to be a tremendous outpouring of love too glorious for any pen or brush to depict. It swept me off my feet, as it were, and carried me into regions far beyond the reach of reason and fancy. No shadow of care, of doubt, of sorrow, or of a question-mark anywhere.

Ah, bliss of sheer being! Bliss of in-breathing and out-breathing life freely, unhurriedly, unconsciously,

120

oblivious of pendulums and clock-arms! Bliss of gath-
ering the worlds into one's heart as gathers the hen
her brood under her wings! Bliss of undivided self!
Bliss of rapturous existence: Ah, bliss of sheer being,
I have tasted you tonight!

Perhaps it was but for a moment; yet it was a
moment worth a whole life-time. Had my life since
birth been a road strewn with pricks and brambles,
but leading to that moment, I should be more than
happy to have walked it and to consider that I have
lived a full life; I should also bless it and bless the
hand that laid it for me and led me to it.

Blessed be forevermore that Life whose surpassing
beauty carries us beyond ourselves.

How do you know, Pitted Face, that the spell of
self-forgetfulness you tasted tonight was not a prelude
to deeper and longer spells terminating in that eternal
ecstasy of selflessness for which you have always been
yearning with all your heart and soul?

Help me, God, to forget myself.


**Saturday**


When the difference between two things or two
phenomena is very vast people compare it to the dif-

ference between heaven and earth. Vaster still is the difference between myself tonight and myself two nights ago.

Two nights ago I was oblivious of Pitted Face, and so I tasted the bliss of sheer being. Tonight I am oblivious of everything in the world except Pitted Face, and have nothing but the taste of bitter bewilderment in my mouth.

How very broad, yet how very narrow is man; how distant, yet how near; how breath-taking swift, yet how terribly sluggish!

I am all perturbance, commotion and chaos today. If anyone asked me the reason, I could give no answer.

I seem like a pot on a mad fire with nothing in it but pebbles; or like a grain of corn in a handful of chaff and dust caught in a whirlwind.

In the past, whenever my serenity was disturbed, I would ascribe it to the division in me between the known and the unknown Pitted Face. Today I seem to be not only one unknown Pitted Face but a multiplicity of unknown Pitted Faces. They peep at me from countless holes, and no two of them are alike; they speak to me a polyglot no word of which I can understand. I feel like a beleaguered fortress with each of those Pitted Faces, quite independently of the rest, doing his utmost to force his way into the fortress and to occupy it ahead of the others. They seem to be racing for the honor, if it be honor.

122

What seek you, besieging host, of this fortress, and what think you are the treasures that await you in it after you have forced it?

You shall not find in its ruins anything more precious than ruins. Nor shall you find in its fireplaces anything more than ashes. The fire itself is still on its way to God.

You shall find in it a handful of years swathed in the darkness of a blind past and the glow of a seeing future; neither are they a total darkness, nor a bright light,—neither a dumb uncertainty, nor an eloquent certainty. Perhaps it is a darkness seeking light, or an uncertainty endeavoring to become a certainty. The name of those years is Pitted Face.

Storm on, ferocious hosts; storm on! Either you break through my fortifications, or I raze yours to the ground.

*Friday*

Alone.

Yes, alone; with no human being to keep me company upon the whole face of the earth. All have perished. The earth is one monster cemetery, grim, for-

lorn and ominously quiet. Nowhere is there a sign of
any biped feverishly seeking with muscle, mind and
imagination to snatch a mouthful of pleasure from the
cupboards of the earth.

Nowhere a mother bearing, delivering, or suckling;
nowhere a babe creeping, lisping, or crying; nowhere
a father working, earning, or building.

Not a ship in any sea, nor in the air; not a car, a
train, nor a caravan on land.

Not an ax in any wood; not a pruninghook in any
vineyard; not a plow in any field.

No chimneys belching smoke; no whir of wheels;
no shrill of whistles.

Not a worshipper in any temple; not a physician
in any hospital; not a scholar in any school.

No poet hunting rhymes; no writer stringing
words; no painter smudging canvas.

Not a peal of laughter; not a sob; not a quiver of
a string or of a vocal chord.

No one to buy or to sell; no one to compete or to
speculate; no one to war or to be warred upon.

All, all have perished, with me left as the sole
witness of their doom. Not earthquakes and floods;
not famine and plague; not beasts and birds of prey
effaced them from the earth; but wars,—their own
wars,—and the pestilences they bring in their wake
were the cause of their extermination.

They perished because of their inordinate greed

and merciless competition for the bounties of the earth. Like ill brought up children invited to a feast, they strove for the largest and choicest morsel and fell in their strife leaving the rich board as richly laden with delectable foods and drinks as ever before. Famished, a-thirst and naked they died, their flesh torn to shreds, their bones ground to dust, their hearts sizzling in the fiercely raging furnaces of their lusts. And, lo! The fountains of the earth are still gushing forth, abundant, inexhaustible.

The earth is still the earth,—the selfsame tender mother feeding her children freely with her flesh and blood. Today as ever in the eons past, she threads her luminous way among the luminous spheres, singing the songs of Yesterday into the ears of Tomorrow; folding the seasons and unfolding them; bearing her burdens with as light a heart as bears the air the vulture and the skylark. Divinely serene she is in her perfect obedience to that omniscient Will which fertilized her vast womb with the germ of life.

Being the sole survivor of the human family, that earth is now all mine. What shall I do with so vast, so rich a heritage!

What shall I do with all the gold and silver and precious stones of the earth? With all the grains, the fruits, the legumes, and the meats? Had I a thousand hands, and mouths, and eyes, and stomachs, and noses, I could consume but an infinitesimal fraction of the incalculably rich stores. What of the fragrance, the beauty and the love of the earth? Is there aught in the universe that could exhaust that fragrance, that beauty and that love?

Arise from your graves, you, ingrates! Arise and ask forgiveness of the earth; for you have denied her, while she denied you not. Arise, for Pitted Face, the sole heir to the earth, is willing and ready to transfer his heritage to you. Take it, take it; it is all yours. But beware, my friends, of dividing it. It is for all of you without exception. The moment you divide it, it divides you. Then you become the heritage, and it, the heir; then you become the possession, and it, the possessor. Beware, my friends, beware how you manage your heritage.

Eat, and drink, and be filled; not alone with the things your own teeth masticate, and your stomachs digest; but also with those things your neighbors masticate and digest. For the fiercest hunger is the hunger of him who would not have his fill save by leaving his neighbor hungry; and the cruelest thirst is that which would not be slaked save by causing another to parch with thirst; and the bitterest death is the death of one who would attempt to sustain his life by undermining other lives, not knowing that thereby he is undermining his own life. For what man's life is not a pillar in the lives of all men? You live by each other; why do you not live for each other? You all suck

126

life from the breasts of the earth. Are you not ashamed to tear up the breasts from which you suck your life!

Alone!

On every side are the ruins of the once mighty and arrogant Civilization. Afflicted with too many blind, yet heady architects, it ended by crashing on the heads of all.

Teeming with memories and alive with fantastic shadows are these ruins; the shadows of wealth in ermine, and of indigence in tatters; of lowliness and pride; of ringing laughter and trickling tears; of dancing pleasures and cringing pains; of faith exultant, and of brazen unbelief; of meek contentment, and of grasping discontent; of hopeful birth, and of hopeless death; of souls sailing down the stream, and souls rowing up the stream.

Deaf, dumb and blind are these ruins; yet but a while since they heard with millions of ears, and spoke with millions of tongues, and saw with millions of eyes. It would seem that all they heard was the voice of death, and all they spoke was self-condemnation, and all they saw was utter desolation. More fitting would it be for them to hear the voice of life, to speak self-exaltation, and to see green meadows, golden fields and prosperous habitations.

Humbled is the haughty one; her nose is in the mire!

127

Prostrate is the overbearing one; her lofty towers are made to bite the dust!

Exposed is the lewd one; she and her lovers are now food for worms!

The erstwhile comely whore is now too hideous for words; her lustful breasts are dripping pus; her lips are cracked and parched; her cheeks are charred and furrowed; her body is covered with boils and stinks unto heaven; so much so that I marvel at the breeze keeping a normal temperature, and at the earth not vomiting its entrails.

Choked is the voice of the temptress, and broken is the flute with whose silver notes she used to entice her lovers into her brothels. Should not the sun sing dirges, and the moon shed tears?

Shattered is the bow and splintered are the arrows with which the great adventuress designed to hunt contentment for her beloved ones, yet hunted them nothing but dreary discontent. Rejoice, you, fishes of the sea. Rejoice, you, birds of the air. Rejoice, you, rams and bullocks, lambs and calves, and all the innocent creatures of the wood and plain. The hand whose greatest sport was to destroy life is now a palsied hand.

Listless, sad and lonely hangs the bloody banner of blood-thirsty Civilization, with no one to trumpet a salute or to offer a fulsome obeisance; for all had given it so freely of their blood until they had no drop to give. Therefore are they now the prisoners of death.

Dead is the harlot; dead all her cheated lovers.

Sleep on, sleep on, sleepless lovers. So furious was your love, it robbed you of the pleasure of sleep.

Sleep on, sleep on, restless lovers. Too busy were you catering to the vagaries of your mistress to taste of real rest. Rest now and give the earth a rest. More mindful and considerate of your comfort is the earth than your own selves. Perhaps when you have rested well you will wake up from your long, deep sleep knowing how generous the earth is, and how good it is to be awake.

Sleep on, sleep on in the dust. Perhaps you will hear and understand what dust communicates to dust.

Sleep on with the ever-wakeful and ever-hungry worms. Perhaps you will hunger for more than worms hunger for; perhaps you will wish to be filled with food other than worms perpetually devour.

Sleep on, sleep on in shrouds of gloom and silence. Perhaps you will come to see the bright heart of night; perhaps you will come to hear the inspiring voice of silence.

Sleep on, sleep on, with sleepless Pitted Face intoning you sweet lullabies.

Sleep on, sleep on, sleep on. . . .

Enough, enough.

A sticky chill creeps through my body and into my heart as I imagine myself the sole human being on the earth. I cherished my solitude and silence when there were people about me whose company I shunned, and whose speech annoyed me. Now that I find myself alone with no one of my own race, my solitude becomes an unbearable loneliness, my silence a stifling dungeon, and my whole existence a dreary detachment. Such a dreariness I never felt before. Heretofore I felt myself a stranger among men, but close to everything else in nature. Now I feel myself a stranger to everything in nature, but close to men.

Is it habit? Is it that my eye, ear and nose have become so accustomed to people that they no longer can live without them? I do not know. I do know that the earth is not the earth without human beings. With them she is a house full of boisterous children. The youngsters play merrily, shout lustily, displace and break things, and turn the house upside down. Yet you feel that the house bubbles with activity and life. It is a living house. Emptied of children, of their noise and boisterous activity, it becomes a dead house.

No! The earth is not the earth without men and their incessant, childish pranks, and noisy games of hide-and-seek; of quarreling over trinkets; of making peace over the body of a cat they all joined in drowning; of loving and hating; of building up and tearing down; of breaking into factions, and of laying plans for the most *exciting* way of killing the next hour. Are not men the children of the earth not yet come

130

of age! They should be judged according to their age.

Alone!

How can I be alone when with me is Night and all that is wrapped in its cloak; and Day with all it unfolds?

How can I be alone when with me is faith in Night and Day, in myself, and in Man ever peering into that which is beyond Man?

\*     \*     \*

I can give no account as to how and whence the vision came to me of the extermination of the human race off the face of the earth with myself as the sole survivor. The vision seized me so completely and so overpowered me that I was impotent to cast it out of my imagination. The result was that I wrote what I wrote.

Now that I have broken loose from the grip of that vision, I ask myself, what or who inspired it? Can anything come to me from nothing?

Is it not possible, Pitted Face, that what you saw was but a glimpse,—perhaps dim,—of the chart of things in the hazy distance? Perhaps a certain power in you, latent as is the spark in the steel and flint, was able to pierce through the thick veils of time and to reveal to you what may appear to some as the creation of idle fancy. What justification is there for your belief and the belief of others that the earth is designed to remain man's dwelling place unto eternity, and that man is destined to remain man until the end of time?

*Tuesday*

I asked my soul today:
"What do you wish, my soul?"
And my soul replied:
"I wish *to know.*"
Again I asked:
"What do you wish to know, my soul?"
And again my soul replied:
*"All things.*"
Said I:
"Why do you wish to know all things, my soul?"
And the response was:
"Because *I would be free of all things.*"
Then I put the question:
"Is not freedom possible without knowledge?"
To which my soul responded with an emphasis:
*"Without knowledge all is slavery.*"
And I queried again:

"Is not life possible without freedom?"
Quick and positive came the answer:
*"Without freedom life is death."*

### Wednesday

Fruitful silence.

### Thursday

Barren silence.

### Friday

Foreboding silence.

### Monday

As I was walking by the sea about two o'clock past
midnight, and just as I turned a dark bend in the road

a motorcar overtook me and stopped a few paces ahead
of me. Two men jumped at me out of the car and began to bind my hands with a rope. When I asked them
what they wished of me, one of them replied in a low,
husky voice: "We want *you*. Don't you dare open your
mouth." At that instant the roar of another motorcar
was heard coming in our direction. The two men
quickly jumped back into their car and drove off in a
hurry leaving me alone and bewildered. The car resembled that of Sennacherib.

Lord, Lord, my God! I have heard and read of
robbers and highwaymen. Are their avenues of living
so tight and so narrow that they cannot broaden them
except by making other people's avenues tight and
narrow? Are they so destitute that they seek riches
from so destitute a man as Pitted Face?

Truly is the world of men a crazy world.


### Sunday


Mysterious, enchanting Twilight all about me! I
bless your mystery and your enchantment.

Like a cloak half-light and half-dark you wrap me
from head to foot. Neither am I in the light, nor in

the dark. Neither am I a glowing day, nor a pitch-dark night.

Tell me, blessed Twilight, is it decreed for Pitted Face to remain forever a connecting link between day and night? Is there no darkness which is entirely devoid of light? Is there no light entirely free of darkness? What, then, is this voice crying within the depth of me and assuring me that somewhere in the dim distance is a Pitted Face who is beyond the reach of days and nights?

Freedom, priceless Freedom! I have caught a glimpse of your beauteous face, and lo, I am blind. And I had a whiff of your aroma, and lo, I am drunk. For your face is lit with a light too dazzling for the eye of Day. And your aroma is of a musk the like of which has never perfumed the heart of Night. Whoever saw your face but once can no longer rest his eyes on any other face. Whoever smelled your fragrance once must plug his nose against all the odors of the earth.

Freedom, take my hand and release me from the grip of nights and days.

**Saturday**

All is lost . . .
Lost is Pitted Face . . .

135

Lost is his serene solitude, and his far-flung world so teeming with dreams.

Lost is the knowledge he sought. Instead of it he found the knowledge which is no knowledge at all, and which is not aware that it is no knowledge,—the knowledge of men's names, pedigrees, positions, ambitions, traditions and conventions.

Today I "know" who I am,—where I was born, who gave me birth, where I lived before, what I did, who were my friends and foes, whom I loved and hated, and by whom I was loved and hated.

Today I remember everything. Would I never remembered a thing.

How happy I was when my memory was blank as to all that!

How strong were my wings when no past pulled me to the ground, and no memories tied my mind and my heart to the earth!

How spacious was my world bounded on all sides by eternity, with me a roving spirit infatuated with the All-Spirit!

But yesterday this coffee house was vaster than the earth and sky. Today the earth and sky are narrower than this coffee house.

Dead is the living Pitted Face, and resuscitated is the dead Pitted Face. The living Pitted Face died the moment he recalled the dead Pitted Face. Shakeeb is risen; dead is Pitted Face.

136

Accursed be Memory wherein nothing is forgotten, nothing is effaced. A curtain may be drawn for a time over this or that, but not a dot or a tittle are ever blotted out.

No matter how thick the curtain, the day invariably comes when the same hand that drew it on will draw it off. The immediate "cause" may be a passing word, or a trifling act.

The "cause" for lifting the curtain off my past was no more than an article in an issue of a Spanish Journal I found today upon my desk. No doubt it was left there by Sennacherib.

Today I "know" you, Sennacherib; I know you as men know men. How I wish I had never come to know you with that kind of knowledge. Would you had remained in my consciousness that very Sennacherib I have come to know and to like in this very coffee house.

You have killed me, Sennacherib.

You have slain me, my brother, my friend, my comrade—Suleiman.

You have dropped me from a great height and left me bruised in body and soul, and gasping for breath.

You have wakened me from a conscious sleep to an unconscious wakefulness.

Should I call God's wrath upon your head? Yea, yea, I should.

But why, why, why? I should rather forgive you with a forgiveness as clean as my love for you, and as

deep as your hate for me. Why should I blame you
when you are but a man like other men? Whereas I
am a man and a *djinnee* at the same time. And how
shall one who is only a man understand another who
is partly man and partly djinn?

How shall a mere human understand why one from
the djinn world may slay his love with his own hand?

I slew her. I slew her. Yes, I slew her . . .

With my own hand I slew her. What have the
others to do with me? How could I otherwise?

It were nobler by far to empty her veins of her
pure and innocent blood than to charge that blood
with the passion of the beast.

I do not blame you, Suleiman. To you a devil a-
stir is better than an angel asleep. With you *honor*
is above love. With me love is above all things.

You have avenged your *honor*, Suleiman. How
terrible the revenge! How pitiable the honor!

You exhumed Pitted Face, brought him back to
life and stabbed him in the heart.

Who shall avenge Pitted Face and his love?

On whom shall Pitted Face pour his vengeance except on himself?

I am the slayer and the slain. With the same hand
I slew her, I slew myself.

Yes, with my own hand I slew my love, for it was
more than my body could feed, and less than my soul
hungered after. And what man is there who knows

better than I what my body can feed and what my soul hungers after? What have men to do with me?

Away, away with you, Pharisees. Keep your hands off Pitted Face. Turn your eyes away. Bridle your tongues.

Draw back. Keep at a distance.

Not dead yet is Pitted Face. No, Pitted Face is not dead.

Where are your arrows? Where is your powder? Where are your bullets?

Arise, Pitted Face, arise! Let not your heart be faint at the sight of the besieging host.

Arise and shout in their ears: "Bring on your arrows, your powder and bullets. I am mist, and my shield is mist. If you can vanquish mist with your arrows, powder and bullets, then you have won the fight. Otherwise the victory is mine, and yours is disappointment and black defeat."

Do not wail, my mother. Do not weep, my father.

Dance, dance, you drops of pure and innocent blood I have shed with my own hand.

Drink in, my heart, the fragrance of the dancing blood.

I'm here, O Fate. Do with me what you will.

And you, Great Love,

Decide for or against Pitted Face,

Pitted Face the slayer,

Pitted Face the slain,

Pitted Face aflame,
And Pitted Face a heap of ashes.
Judge me, Great Love, according to your justice,
Infinite and Infallible!

THE END

# SUPPLEMENT

Below is the translation of the article in the Argentine newspaper referred to in the memoirs, with the glaring headlines omitted. The issue is dated June 26, 1913.

"The capital was shocked this morning by the news of a gruesome, unprecedented crime. We have grown more or less accustomed to hear of thefts, robberies, murders and suicides. But never did we hear of a young bridegroom slaying his charming bride the first night of their honeymoon for no reason except that he loved her too dearly.

"In one of the fashionable suburbs of the capital is a good-sized Syrio-Lebanese colony. In the colony are wealthy business men, prominent manufacturers, noted architects, lawyers, physicians and journalists. They were all very instrumental in building up the suburb and in bringing it to its present flourishing state.

"Most prominent in the colony, both in wealth and social prestige, are the families of Na'man and Harib who have always been known for their very close and very friendly relations. The first consists of a father, a mother and a son in the prime of youth

141

whose name is Shakeeb and who is their sole son and heir. Extremely keen of mind and exceptionally gifted, señor Shakeeb was graduated from the university with very high honors, astonishing his professors and his fellow-students. It is said, however, that he is abnormal in some directions, although of an unblemished character and conduct.

"The Harib family is composed of a widowed mother and two children: Suleiman and Najla. Señor Suleiman is a young architect of prominence. He and Shakeeb Na'man are more attached to each other than two brothers of the same flesh and blood. This friendship between the two young men paved the way for the relations between Shakeeb and Najla which developed in time into an ardent love. The love led to betrothal, and the betrothal to the altar. The wedding was the most magnificent affair ever witnessed by the colony. The two families felt that their cup of happiness was overflowing. As to señorita Najla, all those who knew her alive and saw her dead testify that she was a rare beauty and a rare personality.

"The newlyweds chose to spend the first night of their honeymoon in the capital's most elegant hotel and warned the management that they did not wish to be disturbed by any callers. All of the following day passed, and no one saw the couple in any part of the hotel; nor did any servants report that they were called upon to render them any service. By midnight the

142

management began to entertain some misgivings about the young guests. A porter was sent to knock at the door, but there was no response. Then the police were called.

"Receiving no reply to their repeated knocks, the men of the police forced open the door which was locked from the inside. The sight that awaited them was too horrible for words. On the bed was the beautiful bride, dressed in an elegant night gown of white silk, and stretched out full length. The gown and the bedding were soaked in blood. The bride's throat was slashed from one side to the other. As to the bridegroom no trace was found of him except a small strip of paper on which was written the following:

" 'I slew my love with my own hand, for it was more than my body could feed, and less than my soul hungered after.'

"Upon examination it became clear that the words were written with Shakeeb's own hand. It was also clear that the bride's expensive jewelry and the rest of the luggage of both the bride and the groom were all intact.

"Secret service men, as well as the bride's brother, señor S. N. Harib, are already carrying on a feverish search for the groom who, without any doubt, is the author of the hideous crime. All, however, are at a loss to assign a plausible reason. Nothing seems to suggest, even remotely, any jealousy, or any dispute

or quarrel. On the contrary, everything seems to in
dicate that the couple loved, trusted and respected
each other in the extreme.

"Truly it is a mystifying crime. Even the secret
service men are at a loss to find a clue or a reason. But
they are going on with their search; and we shall report in time to our readers any new findings."

# TO PITTED FACE

Now that I have wiped my pen from your memoirs, Pitted Face, I find myself carried back thirty-three years into the past,—thirty-three years to a day.

Alone I walk the streets of a town which is not my town, and in a land which is not my land. The night is pitch-hearted, wet-eyed and very cold of breath. Wrapped in a cloak of mist, it is bereft of the faintest ray of light.

Aimlessly I wander in the dark without as much as a stick to feel my way about. Though my eyes are open, my heart is tightly shut. It seems to look for something, yet neither knows what it is looking for, nor where to look for it. Were anyone to ask me that night, "Whereto?" I should have been at a loss for an answer. Perhaps to ward off his curiosity, I would have said that I was looking for Dawn.

Night was almost spent when, of a sudden, I beheld a wisp of rays pierce the mist and roll back the darkness from in front of my eyes and feet. A shadow with a lantern was moving in my direction. And you, Pitted Face, were that shadow.

I saluted you warmly, and you returned the salute with equal, nay, greater warmth. On the instant I felt

you to be no stranger to me; and my feeling was well
founded. For you, too, were looking for Dawn in that
dismal night. You had a lantern but no shelter. I had
a shelter but no lantern. And you consented that we
should combine your lantern and my shelter. Whereupon we strode together to my humble dwelling.
Cold, somber and tight, it became, as soon as you
walked into it, warm, light and very spacious,—so
spacious, in fact, as the space.

Nights and days rolled by with you always in my
mind and imagination, speaking things to me which
no tongue had ever spoken to me before, and telling
me tales which no one ever told. Wishing to share with
others the ecstasy of knowing you, I began to record
and to publish some of your tales and sayings.

That was towards the end of the year 1917. Early
the following year the lord of War called me to his
service,—that same lord whom you and I hate with a
holy hatred. But his call was so imperious that I was
forced to obey it. Thus did War tear me away from
my pen and papers, and from your memoirs of which
I had published but an insignificant fraction.*

The war tore me away from your memoirs, but not
from you. For you were my constant and trusty companion on the front and behind it. It was your luminous spirit that helped my youthful heart and mind

---

* This book, started in a small Pennsylvania town in 1917, was inter-
rupted for many years It was finally finished in 1949.

146

to suffer in silence the arrogance of my superiors and the sheepish submissiveness of my fellow soldiers. It was your gentle touch that helped to lighten the crushing weight of the hideous war equipment I had to carry on my shoulders and back.

Safe and unscathed we came out of the great slaughter-house; but the ecstasy I experienced at my first encounter with you came not back to me; therefore my pen did not go back to your memoirs.

Three decades passed, and people began to think that I had entirely forgotten you. Some pressed me for the balance of your memoirs; some gently reminded me of you. But none were keen enough to know that the ties between you and me were more powerful than time, and more enduring than the earth. Nor were there any who could fathom my love for you and your attachment to me. It were better for both of us that men should be incapable of delving deeper into our souls.

Although I knew full well that you did not record your memoirs for publication, I considered it my bounden duty to publish them abroad so that all who seek what you sought might find in them the sustenance I found. As I send them on their way and wipe my pen from them, I am far from sending you away from my mind, or from wiping you out of my heart. I could not do that even if I wished. But far be it from me ever to wish it.

You know, as I know, that these memoirs are but modest tricklings from the vast reservoir of dreams which is your soul. They are but hushed and distant echoes from that harmonious choir of yearning which is your spirit. And since dreams and yearnings must needs be interpreted to men, may you condone this audacity on my part to act as your interpreter.

Peace be with you wherever you may chance to be. "Forgive, but ask no forgiveness!"

Mikhail Naimy,
Biskinta, Lebanon,
October 10, 1949.

CPSIA information can be obtained at www.ICGtesting.com
Printed in the USA
LVOW032334281211

261434LV00016B/137/P